CW01082049

The White Feather

The Talisman - Book VI

The
White
Feather

Michael Harling

vii

Lindenwald **L︱P** Press

To Mitch and Charlie
Without whom there would be no story.

Chapter 1
Thursday, 28 June 2018

Mitch

Summer stretched out before us—weeks of carefree, empty days—but as soon as we left school behind, Mom started acting a little bit crazy, and everyone did their best to ignore it.

Starting on our first day off, she got up early every morning and left the house before Dad went to work. She had never done this before, and she wouldn't tell us why she was doing it. All we knew was, she'd be gone when we got up, and then, an hour or so later, we'd hear her car pull into the driveway, and she'd walk into the house as if there was nothing unusual about it.

If we asked her where she'd been, she'd just say, "Out," in the manner of a surly teenager addressing overly inquisitive parents. That made my brother Charlie and me a little anxious; being surly teenagers was our job. When we asked Dad what she was up to, he'd just sigh and give vague answers that told us he was as much in the dark as we were.

On Thursday morning, a week after it had begun, we all sat silent at the breakfast table, with Mom's absence hanging over us like an oppressive question mark.

Then Dad cleared his throat. "Your mother gets,

um, concerned at this time of year," he said. Then he took a bite of his toast and chewed it thoughtfully. "About you, I mean."

"Well, I don't know why she would," Charlie said, shovelling another spoonful of Corn Pops into his mouth.

Dad sighed. "I don't know why, either, but she does. So, I'm asking you to be kind to her, help keep her calm."

"It's not like we're being mean to her," I said.

Dad put his toast down. "Of course you're not. I just think you should stay, well, close to her."

"That won't be hard," Charlie said. "She's watching us like a hawk these days. Hardly lets us out of her sight."

"Except when she goes off like this," I said. "Where does she go every morning?"

Dad pushed his plate of uneaten toast away. "She says she goes jogging, and I think that's a good thing. It will help relieve her stress."

Dad picked up his briefcase and started for the door. Then he paused, "And please," he said, with his back to us, "I'm begging you, stay away from that cloak."

Charlie dropped his spoon into his empty bowl. "What is her problem with our cloak?"

Dad continued to face the door, but his voice picked up an edge. "Maybe I should be asking you that? You're getting far too old to be playing with it, yet you insist on dragging it out every summer. And it really upsets your mother, so I'm asking you not to."

I kept my mouth shut, but Charlie wouldn't let it go.

"Well, I don't know why we shouldn't. There's—"

Dad spun around, his face red. "I don't know either, and it's driving me crazy. Do you think I like this time of year? Do you think I like seeing her this way? And all because you won't act your ages and stop playing silly games with that cloak."

We both stared at him, too shocked to speak. Charlie's face went white.

Then Dad drew a shaky breath and went on, a little calmer. "I know it's unfair. I know it's your cloak. I know there is no logical reason for it, but I'm begging you, for your mother's sake, for my sake, for this family's sake, just leave it. Okay?"

I kept silent, hoping that Charlie would too. It was our pact, to say nothing and let Dad assume our silence meant agreement. It was the only way we could think of to not break promises. But this time, Dad wasn't having it. He gave us the hard stare and waited us out.

It only took a few seconds for me to crack. "We won't do anything to upset Mom," I said.

"See that you don't," he said, turning back to the door. "And keep close to her."

"But I have a driver's test tomorrow," I said.

Charlie looked up from the table. "And I'm going with him, to apply for my learner's permit."

Dad stopped and sighed. "Then have your mother drive you. It will be easier than taking the bus."

He left then. Seconds later we heard the front door slam.

Charlie rinsed his bowl in the sink and put it in the dishwasher. I followed him, carrying Dad's uneaten breakfast and my own bowl.

"Do you think you can keep your promise?" Charlie asked.

I looked at him. "You mean our promise?"

"You made it."

"For both of us."

Charlie closed the dishwasher. "Well, it doesn't really matter, we've already broken it. These days, there's nothing we can do that doesn't upset her."

"I expect she's already upset. She doesn't leave the house like this because she's happy."

"Where do you suppose she goes?"

"I can't guess, but this started as soon as school broke up, and that worries me."

"Well, at least it makes checking the mail easier," Charlie said. "I suppose you've already been out to look."

"Yes, and that's what really worries me. Nothing came. And tonight is the full moon."

"So, maybe Granddad sent it late, or it got delayed."

I shook my head. "It always comes on the day of the full moon."

The door banged open. We thought it was Dad coming back, having forgotten something, or to have another word with us, but the heavy footsteps crossing the living room weren't Dad's, they were Mom's.

"Where's your father," she shouted as she stomped into the kitchen. She had a small cardboard box in her hand that was covered in stickers and thick, black writing.

"He just went to work," Charlie said.

Mom slammed the box onto the kitchen table. "Well, he's going to hear it when he gets home. And this time there'll be no excuses. Your grandfather has gone too far this time, and your father is going to put a stop to it."

I looked at the box, with its foreign stickers and spidery handwriting. "That's from Granddad."

"You bet it is," she said, her voice rising a pitch. "And look what he's sent you this time."

She pawed through the box, extracting several handfuls of crumpled newspaper. Then, with a triumphant smile that looked more like a grimace, she held up a bullet.

It wasn't a dainty thing, like a shiny .22 calibre, it was huge and menacing, the cartridge casing tarnished with age, the tip tapered to an aggressive point.

"I'm sure it's not live," I said, hoping to calm her down. Instead, her voice went up an octave.

"I don't care if it's live or dead or in a coma, it's a bullet."

The word "bullet" came out an octave higher still. Both Charlie and I winced.

"Well, we didn't ask him to send it," Charlie said.

"I know it's not your fault," she said, in a voice indicating that, yeah, it was our fault. "It's that grandfather of yours."

She slammed the bullet onto the table. Despite my certainty that it wasn't live (Granddad wouldn't be that stupid, would he?) I jumped.

"When your father gets home, he's going to hear about this, and he's going to contact your grandfather and put a stop to this once and for all."

I thought about reminding her that Granddad had still not provided any contact details—no telephone number, no e-mail, no skype, not even an exact address, aside from Horsham, which was the name of the town where he lived—but I decided it wasn't a good idea. She must have seen the intent on my face, however, because she immediately rounded on me.

"I don't care if he has to fly over there and track him down," she screeched, in response to my unspoken comment. "But this stops now."

Leaving the bullet where it was, she stomped across the kitchen and snatched her cedar box off the windowsill. The box had been hers since she'd been a little girl, a gift from her own grandfather. Over the years, it had served as a keepsake box, a jewellery box, a recipe holder, and it now resided on the kitchen windowsill as a catch-all container. She upended it—scattering pens, pencils, loose change, an old bottle of super glue, a broken computer mouse, assorted screws, a tape measure, a pair of scissors, and other bric-à-brac, across the kitchen counter—and scrabbled through the mess, scattering items onto the floor, until she came up with what she was looking for: the key. Then she returned to the table, threw the bullet into the box and slammed the lid.

"There," she said. "Now we just need to wait until your father gets home."

She locked the box, stuffed the key into the pocket of her jeans and sat heavily in the chair Dad had vacated. Her hair was unkempt, her eyes bloodshot and baggy and, although she still seemed upset, it was mixed with triumph and relief. She looked at Charlie and me, and then at the box, and sighed, her shoulders slumping as if all the energy was draining out of her.

"I'm going to lie down," she announced, scooping up the box. "Stay in the house and stay quiet." Then she looked around at the junk scattered over the counters and floor. "And clean up this mess."

She walked out of the room, her footsteps still

loud as she went up the stairs. We heard her go into the bathroom, and then heard a faint rattle that told us she was taking one of her sleeping pills. The doctor had prescribed them the year before, to help her cope with her anxiety. She had taken a few, but then her anxiety had disappeared—coincidentally, the day after Granddad had sent us the glass cutters—and since then, the bottle sat on the second shelf of the medicine cabinet, untouched. Until now.

"So," Charlie said, when silence finally returned, "that's what she's been up to."

"And that's why Granddad's gift didn't come this morning. She's been going to the Post Office and picking up the mail."

"Outsmarted," Charlie said.

I nodded. "Yeah."

The truth was, I hadn't put much thought into it. Her yearly anxiety over the gifts had become a sort of tradition, and I had put so much faith in my plan to get the mail before her—because it had worked so well last year—that it hadn't occurred to me she might find a way around it. And now, the enormity of my mistake began to sink in.

"We're not going to be able to go," I said to the tabletop.

"That's not necessarily a bad thing, is it?" Charlie asked. "I mean, we don't have to go, do we?"

I thought about it. "I don't know. Maybe this was supposed to happen."

I got up and started pacing the floor. Then, just for something to do that might make me feel normal, I began collecting the junk Mom had scattered around.

"Every year, Granddad sends us these gifts," I said, taking a mixing bowl out of the cupboard to load the junk into. "And every year Mom gets upset, and every year we end up getting the cloak—"

"And every year we swear we'll never do it again," Charlie said. "And then we spend the year trying to forget how horrible it was, and every spring we all— Mom, Dad, us—start dreading the beginning of summer because we know it's going to happen again. So, yeah, do we really have to go?"

For the first time since the gifts began, I seriously considered the question. We had never entertained the question before, but we were getting older now, and maybe Dad was right, maybe it was time we grew out of this. I mean, who knew what Granddad was up to over there? And we had never fully convinced ourselves that the adventures were anything more than fanciful dreams, though we never had any other dreams like them.

"I don't suppose we do," I said, testing the words. "I gotta say, I really didn't like the look of that bullet. Maybe we could give this one a miss."

I had hoped to feel relief when I spoke the words, but instead my stomach knotted.

Charlie slouched in his chair, clicking his finger against the empty cardboard box. "Well, at least it looked modern. If we do go, maybe they'll have invented indoor plumbing."

I leaned against the counter. "But modern warfare? We've been lucky with medieval warfare, but I don't think I want to chance running into anything like that bullet."

Charlie scoffed. "We don't even know if these dreams, fantasies, happenings, or whatever, are real."

"But we don't know that they aren't."

For a while, it was so silent I could hear the ticking

of the clock in the living room.

"You know this is going to happen again," Charlie said after a while.

I nodded. "And again."

"And I'm getting tired of upsetting Mom every year, and now Dad's mad at us. Maybe we should just put an end to it. I have better things to do this morning than take a nap and have some stupid dream about going back in time."

I wanted to agree, but there was still that tightening in my stomach, and the unanswered question.

"But what if it is real?"

Charlie shook his head. "You can't be serious."

"Well, we never doubted it before."

Charlie sat up and pushed the cardboard box aside. "We were children," he said, slowly and loudly, as if I was dim. "We're not children anymore, and we're letting Granddad treat us like we're still seven years old. That's probably what he thinks, and we're playing along."

"You don't send bullets to children."

"Who knows," Charlie said. "He's daft enough."

"Daft," I said. "You got that from John."

Charlie slumped back into his chair. "Look, I don't know what to think. Who knows what Granddad has in mind."

"Did he say anything?"

"I don't know," Charlie said, already grabbing for the box. He pulled the rest of the wadded-up newspaper out. "Yeah, there's a note at the bottom." He took it out and shook the folded paper open. "It says, 'Hello-Boys, I found this in that old man's What-Not Shop the other day and thought you'd find it interesting.'"

"That's it?"

Charlie wadded up the note and threw it into the empty box. "Yeah, that's it. Typical." He leaned back in his chair. "It's official now, I'm done with this."

I went back to pacing. "I want to be, I really do, but I can't shake the feeling—"

"C'mon, Mitch," Charlie snapped. "You really can't believe—"

"I don't want to," I said, my voice rising, "but if we don't go, we'll never know. If we go this time, we can settle the question once and for all."

"And how are we supposed to do that?"

I threw my hands up in disgust. "I don't know."

"And why do you want to settle the question in the first place?"

I stopped; my frustration deflated by the question. "I suppose, if we can prove it's real, then we ought to keep going."

"It seems to me," Charlie said, "that if it is real, we should stop going. I don't mind taking the chance of getting killed in a dream, but real life?"

"But, if we are really going back in time, then don't you think that makes us special? And the adventures more than adventures. If it's real, it must be for some purpose."

"So, you want to keep going if it's real, and I want to keep going if it's a dream. That seems fair. Now how do we decide that?"

I sat at the table and cradled my chin in my hands. "Help me think. What do we know, and how can we use it?"

"We know we always show up in the same place," Charlie said.

"And we know that, this time, it's relatively modern. More so than last time, even. And that means we'll be in recent, verifiable history."

"What of it? If we buried something, or built something, or mark something, we'd have to go to England to see it."

We thought some more.

"Newspapers," I said. "The Internet is full of newspaper archives. We could go into town, find a shop that sells papers and look at the date and the headlines. Then, we could come straight back and check to see if the newspaper we saw matched the real one."

"That seems kinda iffy."

"Then we'll check a few newspapers. National and world news. We can look at some of the articles about what is happening in the country and the world at the time. Even if the actual papers aren't on the web, the events might be."

Charlie kept silent.

"C'mon," I said. "It could work, and it's our only chance. And I promise. If we can't get proof, we'll just forget about it, and Mom can stop worrying and Dad can stop being so on edge and we—"

"That's all well and good," Charlie said, "but you're forgetting something—no matter what we decide, we still can't go."

My head sank closer to the table.

"Mom's got the bullet," Charlie continued. "And once Dad gets home and she shows it to him, that will be the end of it. He's going to go mental. I mean, did you see that thing, it's not like the quills or the glass cutters. A bullet can't mean anything but trouble."

11

I thought about it. Charlie was right, this was the end. There would be no adventure, now or ever again. Dad would have to contact Granddad somehow, and any future gifts would be stopped, intercepted, or confiscated, which, to tell the truth, would be no big deal. Unless, of course, it really was real.

"Then we've got to find a way," I said.

Chapter 2

Charlie

I shook my head. "How? We can't get the box, and even if we could, we can't open it to get the bullet."

"Then we'll take the box," Mitch said, getting to his feet. From his tone, I knew there would be no talking him out of it. "We don't need to open it. Mom took a sleeping pill. Remember when she did that last year? It knocked her out for hours. We can sneak the box out of her room, do a quick reconnaissance trip, and put it back when we're done. She'll never know."

I sighed. "We are going to get so grounded over this."

We did our usual prep, which included emptying our pockets (although this wasn't strictly necessary, because nothing ever came into the past with us beside our clothes and the gift) and changing into more versatile clothes. Being summer, we were wearing short sleeved shirts, but we didn't know what we might be getting into, so we each put on a long-sleeved shirt and a light jacket. Then we went and got the cloak.

Mom had folded it carefully and put it in the back of her closet. It was nerve wracking getting it out, but not as nerve wracking as taking the box, which she had on the bed next to her, with her fingers resting against it.

I pulled it away, slowly, all the while expecting her eyes to pop open, but she didn't wake up. Even when the bullet rolled and clanked against the inside of the box, making us both jump, she didn't move; she just continued to lay there, breathing even, shallow breaths.

Then we went to Mitch's room. He laid on his bed, pulling the cloak over himself, but I waited, holding the box.

"What?" Mitch asked, when I didn't join him.

"Before we go," I said, "I need you to promise three things."

"I've already said we're only going—"

"You've promised things before."

"Well, they were out of my control."

He had a point, but I wasn't letting it go.

"Promise me that we are only going for a quick look, that we will not go to Pendragon's house, and that we will not go looking for any adventures. Just in and out. No excuses."

"I suppose, yeah, I can do that."

I spit on my hand and held it out to him.

"Swear."

"What, are we twelve years old?"

"Swear."

Reluctantly, he spit on his hand, and we shook.

Then I laid down next to him, with the box on my chest. Mitch spread the cloak over us, and we waited.

And waited.

"This isn't going to work," I said, after half an hour had gone by. "We'll still be lying here when Dad gets home."

"There's got to be a way," Mitch said, flinging the

cloak aside.

I sat up. "I know, let's put the box back and cover Mom with the cloak. She can go."

"Very funny."

"Well, I can't sleep. I'm too keyed up."

"Mom was pretty keyed up," Mitch said, "and she's sleeping."

He looked at me, and we both had the same thought.

"No way," I said.

"We could cut one in half, take a half dose each."

"That's still not—"

"C'mon," he said, jumping off the bed.

He got one of Mom's sleeping pills from the bathroom and, downstairs in the kitchen, used a steak knife to cut it in two. Then we each took a half and went back to the bedroom.

"I don't know," I said, when we were back under the cloak, "I still don't feel tired."

"Give it time," Mitch said. "Count sheep, or something."

I kept still, breathing slowly, feeling the weight of the box on my chest.

"We are going to get so grounded over this," I said again, as I slowly began to sink.

Tumbling toward sleep, I felt the familiar fear and excitement begin to rise. I pushed them aside and sank deeper.

Chapter 3
Friday, 25 August 1916

Mitch

A hot wind, a roar, and a jolt like a short, sharp earthquake. The bed lurched, spilling me onto the floor. Charlie landed on top of me, flailing and shouting.

We were tangled in the cloak. I yanked at it, pulling it off me. It was dark. The roar dropped to a rumble, but the floor continued to vibrate. Around me, in the dark, I heard ominous creaking, then thuds and thumps as heavy objects fell from above and hit the floorboards. Every thud made my teeth rattle. The air was thick with dust. I smelled smoke, and gunpowder.

"The box!" Charlie's voice. He struggled out of the cloak. "I can't find the box."

"It's got to be here," I said. "But—"

"What just happened?"

"I don't know."

"And why's it so Dark?"

"I don't kn—"

And then it wasn't dark. A blaze of flame shot up some distance from us, illuminating everything. We were in a house, or what used to be a house. Next to us, a stone fireplace was still standing, but around the room, broken beams jutted at unnatural angles, and brick walls, lit by the fire, ended in ragged edges, showing black sky beyond.

We were sprawled on a floor made of rough, uneven wood, covered in grit and broken bits of stone. I scrabbled around in the debris.

"We've got to find the box," Charlie said.

I shook my head, my mind foggy and my ears ringing. "We've got to get out of here."

From outside came distant shouts, drawing nearer and more urgent.

"C'mon," I shouted.

"The box," Charlie said.

Around us the house creaked. Another beam fell. The flames danced higher. Then, amid the bricks and dust and smoke, I saw a glint of metal.

"There," I said.

Charlie dove for it.

"It's the bullet," he said, stuffing it into his pocket. "But where's the box?"

I grabbed him by the shoulders and shook him. "Who cares. We need to get out of here."

I scooped up the cloak and we made our way through the gloom, toward the shouting, ducking under beams and scrambling over chunks of broken walls. The fire began to crackle as the beams caught. Smoke stung my eyes and burned my lungs.

Charlie coughed. "There's a door ahead."

Beyond the door we heard people shouting.

"Get water!"

"Bring blankets!"

"Is anyone inside?"

The door thudded and bowed inward as someone tried to break it down.

Then I heard the screaming.

"There's someone else in here," I shouted to

Charlie.

"But where?"

The screaming continued.

"Above us. Find the stairs."

We went back into the smoke, feeling our way. In front of me, Charlie hacked and coughed and tripped. "Ow! I found the stairs."

We felt our way up, toward the screaming.

"Come this way," I shouted.

The screaming stopped. We heard footsteps thudding on the stairs. Halfway up we bumped into someone. A woman, in a nightgown. She grabbed us each by an arm and tried to pull us upstairs. "My baby, my baby."

"Where?"

"Up there. I couldn't get to her."

From below we heard the door crack. We grabbed the woman and dragged her downstairs. She flailed and tried to pull away. "No, no, my baby, my baby."

The door burst open. Several people poked their heads in. We shoved the woman toward the doorway.

"Take her," I shouted.

The woman struggled and screamed. "My baby."

A man wearing a flat cap and a canvas jacket grabbed her.

"My baby, my little girl," the woman sobbed, beating him on the chest with her fists. "She's upstairs."

"We'll get her," I said.

Inside the house, another beam fell. Heat from the fire belched toward us like a blast furnace.

"No," the man said, hugging the woman in his brawny arms, "it's too late, there's nothing to be done."

"Hold her," I said to the man. "Don't let her follow us."

We ran back to the stairs. The heat was worse than the smoke now. I threw the cloak over both our heads and we ran, side by side, up the stairs. At the top we tripped over a beam and sprawled on the floor. Behind us, another beam fell, crashing through the stairs. I held my breath, waiting for the upper floor to collapse. It trembled but stayed together. Around us, boards creaked, the fire crackled and, somewhere nearby, a baby howled.

We were on a small landing, an open doorway to our right. Smoke billowed through the opening, and flames crackled inside the room. My throat clenched with smoke and panic, and I feared we were too late. The howling sounded again, and Charlie pointed to the left, at another door, hanging open, held to the frame by a single hinge. "She's over there." Jumping up, he ran to the open door and stopped abruptly on the threshold, nearly toppling into the room.

"Whao!"

I ran to him. Just beyond the door the floor disappeared. We stared down into flames. From the other side of the hole, the baby shrieked again. She was sprawled on what was left of the floor, next to a crib that had toppled over.

"That's why she couldn't get the baby," I said.

"Well, neither can we."

The baby couldn't crawl, but she arched her back and flailed her arms, trying to turn over, and each movement took her closer to the edge.

I looked around. The stairs were gone, the room behind us was in flames, the only way out was the small window in the baby's room. We had to get over the hole.

"The door," I said.

We wrenched the door, snapping the remaining hinge out of the frame. Then we set it on the threshold and let it fall forward. Its top edge slammed down on the floorboards near the baby.

"Just big enough," Charlie said.

He stepped on the edge. It creaked but held. He took another step, and another. The door cracked. He lunged forward, landing half on the boards, and scrambled to safety. The door still spanned the hole, but it hung down in the middle, its spine snapped. Behind me the flames roared, and heat seared my back.

"The cloak," Charlie shouted. "Throw me an end."

I pulled it off the floor, grabbed a corner and threw the other to Charlie. He grabbed it and held. Behind him, the baby squirmed closer to the edge.

"The baby!"

"You first," Charlie said. "On three."

"One, two," we both counted. "Three."

I jumped forward. Charlie pulled. My foot hit the middle of the door. It held for moment, then snapped, but it was long enough for me to push forward as Charlie yanked me into the room. I landed half on the boards as the broken door tumbled into the flames below. Charlie grabbed my arms and helped me scramble onto the floor. Then he grabbed the baby.

Fire lapped into the landing where we had just been, and the floor beneath my feet became hot.

"Quick," Charlie said.

I threw the cloak to him. "Wrap the baby in this."

I picked up the small crib and, holding it by one

leg, swung it against the window. The glass shattered; the wood splintered. I swung again. And again. The crib broke to pieces. I grabbed one of the legs, smashed out any remaining glass and stuck my head out the window.

"Over here," I shouted.

Men and women came running around the side of the building. Just a few, then five, seven, ten. They gathered below the window. I took the baby, now thoroughly bundled inside our cloak.

"I'm going to throw the baby out," I shouted. "Catch her!"

The crowd surged forward. I leaned out as far as I could and let the bundle drop. They caught her easily. The only danger to the baby was of her being smothered by her rescuers.

"Move away," I shouted, as I climbed out the window.

I looked below. The crowd began to pull back. I jumped, hit the ground with a thud and rolled. I lay still for a moment, breathing the cool, fresh air, then coughed.

Charlie thudded down next to me.

Hands pulled us to our feet. Arms held us while we coughed and hacked, and we all made our way to the street. People hugged us, gave us water, a woman nearly broke my neck as she wrapped her arms around me and said, "Thank you," over and over.

The small house was fully aflame now. What remained of the roof collapsed with a roar, sending a geyser of sparks high into the night sky, then, one by one, the walls caved in. We both stared at it in growing disbelief.

"So much for a quick trip," Charlie said.

Chapter 4

Charlie

The crowd, which numbered about thirty people, swarmed around the woman and her baby, taking turns hugging her while she cried. People crowded around us too, shaking our hands, patting our backs, and saying things like, "Well done," and calling us heroes. No one was fighting the fire. There was no point.

"We need to get out of here," I said.

Mitch shook his head. "We need our cloak."

Then the man with the flat cap and canvas jacket, the one who had broken the door down and who we had handed the woman to, came toward us. He was accompanied by a woman with grey hair and a shawl wrapped tight around her. Between them was the woman from the house, sobbing, dishevelled, and hugging her baby, still wrapped in our cloak.

"There's naught to do here," he said, "best come with us."

"Um, sure," I said. I looked at Mitch. He shrugged.

"Agnes will see to you," the man said, indicating the woman in the shawl.

Agnes smiled at us. She seemed friendly enough, but I still wasn't sure I wanted to go to where she was taking us. She laid a hand on the sobbing woman's

22

arm. "Edith and the babe need comfort and rest," she said. "You'll want to be with her. You are kin?"

I looked at her, puzzled. "No."

"Then why were you in the house?" the man asked.

"We weren't," I said. "We were just passing by. We saw the fire and went in to see if we could help."

Agnes looked at me. "The fire? What about the bomb? Did you see the Zeppelin?"

"The door was locked," the man said. "We had to break it down."

Edith waved a hand in our direction. "I don't know these boys," she said between sobs and coughs. "But they saved me. And they saved my baby."

"Zeppelin?" Mitch asked.

"It opened for us," I said, striving to keep the guilt out of my voice. "It must have jammed."

"That seems unlikely," the man said, rubbing his chin.

"Leave it be, Frank," Agnes said. "I won't hear a word said against them. And neither will anyone else." She looked at us. "If you're not staying with Edith, then where are you staying?"

"We're not staying anywhere," I said. "I told you; we were just passing by."

"On our way to Horsham," Mitch added.

Frank folded his arms across his chest. "This late at night, on your way to Horsham, out on this road?"

"We must have got lost in the dark," I said.

Frank gave us the look Dad gives us when he knows we're lying. "And you just happened to be standing out here when the raid happened?"

I sighed and looked at Mitch. "The raid?"

The three of them stared at us.

"You're American?" Agnes asked.

Frank cocked his head. "What are you doing—"

"Travelling," I said.

"Vagrants," Frank said.

"They're not—," Edith said, but she started choking and sobbing then, and hugging our cloak, which I assumed still had a baby somewhere inside it.

"That ends it," Agnes said. "You're coming to ours. We'll give you a bed for the night and some breakfast. You can decide where to go in the morning."

She put an arm around Edith's shoulder and guided her away from the crowd. Frank growled but followed, and we followed our cloak.

Chapter 5

Mitch

Agnes and Frank lived at the farm across the lane from the burning building. Five Acre Farm, Frank called it, consisting of a barn, a scattering of outbuildings and a large farmhouse.

When we entered, Frank lit a kerosene lamp and Agnes offered us tea. While the kettle boiled on the blackened wood stove, she fussed over Edith and hunted up two ill-fitting night dresses. By that time, the panic and excitement had worn off and both Charlie and I were ready to drop, so she led us by candlelight to an upstairs bedroom and left us in the dark.

There, we fumble out of our sooty, smoke-smelling clothes and into the strange pyjamas. Charlie took the bullet out of his pants pocket and put it under his pillow, noting that it was the only thing we had left, having lost access to our way home and, temporarily at least, our cloak.

I would have agreed with him, but as soon as my head hit the pillow, I fell asleep.

Minutes later, it seemed, I was awakened by sudden sunlight hitting my face. Squinting against the glare, I saw Agnes drawing the curtains back from an open window. The angle of the sun told me it was late morning, and the faint whiff of smoke told me the house across the lane was still smouldering.

"It would be a good thing for you to be up and dressed sharpish," she said, when she saw me looking at her. "There's a tub waiting for you in the parlour, and food in the kitchen. You'll have time for a wash and a bite to eat, but not much more."

As she left, I shook Charlie awake.

"Wha—?"

"Get up. We need to go."

"Why?"

"I don't know, but Agnes sounded like we ought to be in a hurry."

Charlie rolled over and climbed out of bed. "Hey, my clothes are gone. And yours too."

"Hopefully, they'll be down by the tub. We do need a bath, your hair is more black than red."

"So is yours," Charlie said.

I ran a hand through my hair. It came away covered in ash.

We crept downstairs, where the smell of smoke was replaced with the scent of fresh bread and bacon. It was coming from the kitchen, but we went the other way, into the room we hoped was the parlour. There we found a dented copper tub, half filled with water, sitting by a cold fireplace. Neatly folded on a nearby chair were two towels and some clothes, but they weren't ours.

"Are we meant to wear these?" Charlie asked.

"I guess so," I said, pulling off my nightgown. "But we need to get clean first. And we don't have much time."

"What's the rush."

"I don't know, but Agnes wants us to hurry."

The water was lukewarm. I did a quick soak, used

a bar of coarse soap on my hair and gave Charlie a turn. The water was nearly black, but he washed without complaint. The clothes were sturdy—canvas pants and flannel shirts—worn but carefully mended, and they fit us well. Charlie put the bullet in his pocket, and we went to the kitchen.

It was large and warm, with a wooden table and chairs at one end, the black stove at the other, and cabinets and shelves in between, all laden with glass jars, a few tin cans, and baskets of vegetables. The only person there was Agnes, and the only sound was the sizzling of meat in a cast iron frying pan.

"Sit," Agnes said, scooping the contents of the pan onto two plates.

We sat at the table, and she brought us each a plate of sausages, thick slabs of meat that smelled like bacon, and something that looked like a biscuit.

"Only water to drink. No coffee available, and most of our milk goes for sale. Not much left to us. No butter for your scone, either."

"That's fine, Ma'am," I said, uncertain how to address her.

Agnes laughed. "No need for such formality, young man. You can call me Agnes. But if you run into Frank, best call him Mr. Shaw."

I nodded. "We will, Agnes."

We ate in silence for a few moments, with Agnes sitting at the head of the table, watching us.

"Are you going to let me call you Young Man, or are you going to introduce yourselves?"

"Um, Mitch," I said. "And the one stuffing his face is Charlie."

"Hey," Charlie said through a mouthful of sausage, "I'm hungry."

"But our clothes," I said. "And our … blanket."

Agnes sighed, but not from frustration or impatience. I got the impression she was buying time to put her thoughts together.

"They're safe," she said, after a few seconds of silence. "But I don't know about you."

"What do you mean?" Charlie asked.

Agnes sighed again.

"Had your arrival been different, if you had simply been walking down the road, Frank would have welcomed you in, offered room and board in exchange for working the farm, and everyone would have been happy."

I put my fork down and looked at her. "It wasn't that simple, though, was it?"

She shook her head. "You were in Edith's house. I don't know if she let you in, or if you got in somehow, but you were not wandering down the lane at two o'clock in the morning and just happened to be there when the bomb hit."

I took a bite of egg and chewed it letting the silence stretch out.

"It's complicated," I said.

Agnes nodded. "That it is. Edith insists you were not in her house when she locked up. She claims you appeared out of the smoke, that you came to save her and her baby girl. She says you are angels."

I looked at Charlie, who rolled his eyes.

"Um, we're not," I said.

"I can see that, but you're something."

"We're travellers," Charlie said.

"From where?"

When neither of us answered she continued.

"You might know I washed your clothes, and the

blanket you rolled the baby in."

"Thanks," I said, looking at my plate.

"Your clothes were very strange, but the blanket, well, it's a cloak, isn't it?"

I nodded.

"And it's very old. Ancient, even. So, what are you doing with it, and why are your clothes so different, and what is polyester, tumble-dry, and Wal-Mart?"

"It's—"

She held up her hand to stop me.

"Complicated. Yes, I understand. You are different, and you are here for some reason that you don't wish to admit to. But I see no malice in you, and I am one for letting sleeping dogs lie. Frank, though, he'll be at you like a dog on a bone. And if he can't make your story add up, he'll set the law on you, and I'm not having that. There's enough suspicion around these days without pillorying two young lads for saving someone's life."

She picked up our empty plates and took them to the sink, where she worked the handle of a pump to fill it with water.

"You'll blend in well enough wearing my Jimmy's clothes. And if you are angels, like the widow Pike claims, maybe you'll bring him a bit of luck."

We both stood but stayed next to the table.

"What about our cloak?" Charlie asked.

Before Agnes could answer, and angry voice came from the hallway.

"Agnes Shaw, I am not a widow!"

Agnes turned and the woman we had rescued— Edith—came into the kitchen, carrying her baby, still wrapped in our cloak. She stopped when she saw us, her eyes wide, her lips turned up in a serene smile.

"They are angels," she said. "They came to save me and Verdy, and bring my Tom home." She glared at Agnes. "My Tom, who is still alive."

Agnes, her lips pressed into a thin line, nodded.

"Verdy?" Charlie asked. "Is that your baby's name?"

Edith looked down at her baby, invisible in the folds of our cloak. "She was named after the battle where her father went missing."

Charlie shook his head. "The battle of Verdy?"

"Verdun," Agnes said. Then added in a more sombre tone. "There were many babes named Verdun after that battle."

"But those were for the men who were killed," Edith said. "Verdy's name is a beacon, so Tom will find his way back to us." She looked at me. "And these angels, they have come to help. They will see that Tom finds his way."

I gave her a tentative nod, then looked at Agnes.

"You've done a great thing," she said, looking at me and Charlie. "After the battle, after the baby, Edith wouldn't leave the house. I feared she would pine and leave the poor babe motherless, but you've given her hope. And where there is hope there is healing."

She glanced toward the door, then back at us.

"For that, you deserve our thanks, not our suspicion. So, whatever it is you have come for, you'd best get to it."

"But, our cloak, our clothes?"

"I'll keep them safe, and secret," Agnes said, coming toward us. "When you are ready, come back for them." She ushered us into the hallway and out the front door.

As we stepped onto the porch, we heard a door slam. Agnes looked toward the rear of the house.

"That will be Frank," she said, her voice low and hurried. "Get out now, while you can."

Chapter 6

Charlie

We hurried away from the farmhouse, worried that Mr. Shaw might come after us. Across the road, milling around the smouldering ruin that used to be a house, were about two dozen people, gaping at the destruction. Blending in sounded like a good idea, so we joined them.

Most of the people in the crowd were dressed like us, though there were a few men in suits, some carrying boxy contraptions that I assumed were cameras because they were pointing them at the remains, fiddling with them, then pointing them in a different place and fiddling some more. The other people clustered in small groups, staring and shaking their heads, with worried looks on their faces.

"We appeared next to that fireplace," Mitch said. "So, there's no reason we can't get back home."

I looked to where he was pointing. In the centre of the burned-out house, a stone fireplace remained standing, surrounded by criss-crossed and blackened beams that were still smoking.

"Yeah," I said. "We could crawl through the wreckage and get to the fireplace, if it wasn't about a million degrees in there."

"It will cool down at some point, and when it does, we can get our clothes and the cloak back and go home."

I shook my head. "That's gonna take days."

"So, what do we do in the meantime?"

"Lay low."

"How?"

"By not going to Pendragon's and not looking for any adventures."

I didn't know how we were going to do that, and Mitch didn't ask. We just stood, silent, looking at the ruined house where we, and Edith and Verdy, nearly met a fiery end. Then we noticed that people were no longer staring at the wreckage. Instead, they were looking at us, pointing, and whispering.

"It's them," I heard one of the closer groups say. "They're the lads. The ones who saved Edith."

I turned and saw that one of the men in suits was pointing his camera at us, and another one, with a notebook in his hand, coming our way.

"We need to leave," I said.

Mitch glanced around. "They must be reporters."

"That's all we need," I said, but Mitch wasn't there. He was already walking away. I turned and followed.

We went to the lane and walked as fast as we could without running. From behind, I heard someone call out, "Lads, could I talk to you?"

We ignored him and walked faster. When we got to the little village of Broadbridge Heath, we stopped to catch our breath.

"Did he follow us?"

Mitch glanced over his shoulder. "I don't think so. Looks like we lost him."

I looked around. There were a few people in the village, and others on the road, either walking or riding in horse carts, and none of them were paying any attention to us. It seemed we were, for the time being at least, safe.

"What now?" I asked.

Mitch Shrugged. "We could do what we planned. Go into town and look for a newspaper. With more people around, we'll be less conspicuous. And no one knows us there, so we should be okay."

The road to Horsham, I was pleased to discover, had been paved. It wasn't perfect—mostly cobbles and something that looked like blacktop—but it wasn't the rutted, muddy mess it usually was. The last time I had seen it that smooth had been during the Roman time, and it amazed me to think that it took them nearly two thousand years to re-learn how to pave a road.

"What year do you think this is?" I asked.

Mitch stared ahead for a while, thinking. "I don't know. It seems modern, but not that modern."

"They're still using candles and riding horses, so it can't be much later than when we were here the last time."

"But something dropped that bomb on us. When did they start using bombers?"

Mitch shook his head. "Don't know. World War Two, maybe?"

"That's too modern," I said. "Surely they weren't using horses then."

"I guess we'll have to hope we can find some answers when we get to Horsham."

The road took us past fields and a few small farms, but soon houses began appearing, and some shops. Then we passed the Green Dragon Pub and entered the town.

In the past, the street was muddy and smelled like an open sewer, but now it was paved and teeming with people, horse-drawn carts, bicycles, and even a few antique cars and trucks, chugging and beeping and backfiring. And the town itself was more built up than the last time we saw it, with fewer wooden structures and more buildings made from brick or stone. It was noisy and confusing but at least it didn't smell like a sewer. Instead, it stank of horse manure mixed with the reek of car exhaust.

Men, dressed in suits and wearing bowler hats or wearing clothes like ours with flat caps, and women in wide-brimmed hats and puffy, broad-shouldered dresses, clustered around the fronts of the shops, talking in loud voices, and using a lot of hand gestures. We walked slowly past, listening, hoping for some clues, but all they talked about were bombs and Zeppelins and what the Government should do about it. We eavesdropped until we reached the end of the street and didn't pick up anything of value.

"Maybe we'll have better luck in the town square," Mitch said. "There's bound to be someone there selling newspapers or magazines, something, anything with a date on it."

Turning the corner, we dodged around a cart and sidestepped some workmen carrying a ladder and a bucket of paint, and entered the open area in the centre of town they call the Carfax. But we didn't find any newsstands, or even anyone reading a paper. What we did find was pandemonium.

In the middle of the Carfax stood an octagonal bandstand—covered by an ornate, wooden roof and ringed by a wrought iron fence, all painted blue and white—and throngs of people were gathered around it, forming a crowd so thick it blocked traffic. A tangle of horses, carts and angry drivers clogged the roads. The drivers yelled and shook their fists, but the crowd ignored them. They were all watching a tall, slim man, who was standing on the bandstand waving a large piece of paper over his head.

For such a slim man, he had a big voice. Even standing at the edge of the crowd we could hear him shouting about the Zeppelins. His words cut through the rumble of the crowd, and soon everyone was listening to him.

"Who's next?" the man shouted. "How much longer are we going to let this go on? Do you want to continue to go to bed each night wondering if you, or your loved ones, are going to wake up in the morning?"

His voice rose to a crescendo. He waved the paper. The crowd near the bandstand roared, "No!"

"I have here a petition to the Government," he said, holding the paper higher. "A petition to join other petitions from across the country. A petition to tell the Government we are tired of being bombed and we want out of this war!"

The crowd roared again. The man waved the paper. "Who's with me? Come and sign."

People surged forward. Several more men and women joined him on the bandstand, each with papers, all of them bending over the railing, collecting signatures from the crowd. Some of the cart drivers left their carts and bulled their way into the throng to sign, as well.

But not everyone agreed with him. At the edge of the crowd, near where we were, others began to shout.

"Cowards," they called, pointing to the people signing the papers.

"You are betraying the brave soldiers at the front," others shouted. "Shame on you."

"We have a right to feel safe in our beds," the man shouted back, "but the Government doesn't care about you, and they can't do a thing about the German juggernaut."

Mingled in with the crowd, and making their way toward the bandstand, was a group of women. They weren't chanting or booing or signing the petitions. They were handing out leaflets to the men, who dropped them on the ground without looking at them. All the women were wearing purple, green and white striped ribbons, as if they had won a contest that gave out purple, green and white instead of blue for first prize.

We weren't sure what it was all about, but we knew we weren't going to find a newsstand, so we decided to head back to West Street. When we turned, Mitch bumped into a girl wearing an absurdly large hat and one of those purple, green and white ribbons. She grabbed Mitch's hand, put something in it, and curled his fingers over it so he wouldn't drop it. Mitch raised his hand and opened his fist to reveal a white feather resting on his palm.

Chapter 7

Mitch

The feather was white, delicate, and fluffy, the kind you'd find in a pillow. I looked at the girl. Her hair hung down in ringlets from beneath her hat, resembling rolls of newly minted pennies. A smattering of freckles ran up her nose and across her cheeks just under her green eyes. Her lips were pressed tight, and a vertical line formed between her eyebrows.

"Thank you," I said.

Her eyes narrowed, which made her freckled nose scrunch up. "You're not supposed to thank me," she said.

"Well, what am I supposed to do?" I asked. "You just gave me a gift."

Her mouth dropped opened, then closed. "It's not a gift," she said. "It's to show that you're a coward. You …" she pointed at me, then at Charlie, "and you. Cowards, and you should feel ashamed."

"But we haven't done anything," Charlie said.

She clenched her fists, and her face went red enough to match her hair. "That's just it," she said, "you haven't joined the army, you haven't gone off to fight."

"Well, why would we want to do that?" Charlie asked.

"I'll tell you why you won't," the girl said, her voice rising, "because you're cowards, that's why."

I was trying to think of a reason why she was so angry when a man walking nearby stopped, looked at us, and rushed over.

"Is it you?" the man asked, bumping the girl aside. "It is you! I just want to say, 'Well done, well done.'" He shook my hand vigorously, then Charlie's. "You will never meet anyone braver than these two lads," he said, turning to the girl. "Proper heroes, they are. Put on a good show for us last night. Rescued that woman and her baby from the bombed house as it was burning down around them." He shook our hands again. "Good show, lads, good show." Then, as abruptly as he came, he left.

The girl gaped at us. "That was you?"

I nodded and the girl turned red again, only this time she was blushing.

"I suspect you don't support woman's suffrage, though. Do you?"

She folded her arms across her chest and glared as if she was challenging me.

"That's crazy. Why would I?"

"Ha," she said. "I thought not."

"I don't support suffering for anyone," I said, becoming confused. "Women, men, animals, even."

The girl rolled her eyes and shook her head, making her curls swing. "Not suffering, you dolt. Suffrage. Do you think women should vote?"

"Of course they should. Women have a civic duty, just like any else."

Once again, the girl's mouth fell open.

"What?" Charlie asked. "Do you not want women to vote? Is that your thing?"

The girl turned red again, but I wasn't sure if she was angry or embarrassed.

"I … you …"

I held up the feather. "Can I keep this? Even if I'm not a coward?"

Charlie smirked. "Can I get a feather too?"

"You're not in uniform," the girl sputtered. "So, you're still cowards."

I shrugged. "We're not in uniform because we're only seventeen—"

"You could volunteer."

"And I don't think your country would want Americans in their uniform."

"Americans?" But it wasn't the girl who asked. It was another man, standing nearby who had been, up until then, booing the man on the bandstand. He didn't wait for a response; he and his friends grabbed me and Charlie by the shoulders. "Why isn't your country in the war?" he demanded. "It's your lot who are giving the likes of him an audience."

He pointed at the skinny man, who was still encouraging people to sign his petition.

"Well, we will join," I said. "I promise."

"When?" the man holding Charlie asked.

"I don't know," Charlie said, "but they will, honest."

The man turned and looked toward the bandstand. "You don't need to convince me. You need to convince that lot, before they bring this country to shame."

The booing around us intensified and the man on the bandstand responded by chanting, "No more war! No more war!" The people crowding around him picked it up. Soon, the booing and the chanting made it all but impossible to hear. I looked around. The girl had left and was standing with a group of women wearing the same type of ribbon that she had on. They were booing along with the men surrounding us but, nearby, other women were chanting, "No more war!"

I wracked my brain, trying to guess what year it was, and remember when the US joined the war. I knew it was near the end, but when was that? I should have paid more attention in history. All I knew for certain was that Germany lost, and I thought it would be important to keep things that way.

"You can't drop out of the war," I said. "Germany will win. Do you want that?"

"Don't tell us," the man said, "tell them."

"Like they're going to listen," Charlie said.

The man holding me grinned. There was no humour in it, however. "Well, you lads seem to have big mouths. I'm sure you'll find a way."

My feet left the ground as the man lifted me. Another man grabbed Charlie. Then their companions formed a wedge, and they all bulled their way through the crowd, shouting and pushing. The booing women, and more men, followed. The lead men pushed the petitioners out of the way, climbed the stairs to the bandstand, and surrounded the skinny man.

"You can't do this," he shouted as they grabbed him. "Someone call the police."

"Just like a coward," the man holding me shouted, "begging someone else to fight your battles for you."

"I have a right to speak," the man said, struggling to free himself.

"So do these lads."

My feet hit the boards. They plunked Charlie down next to me and stepped back, leaving us exposed to the crowd. Half of them seemed to be on our side, but the other half looked like they wanted to tear us apart.

"Tell them," one of the men shouted at me, "tell them America will enter the war, tell them we don't have to run like beaten curs."

Roars of approval and disapproval rose around us. I looked at Charlie. "When did America enter the war?"

He shrugged. "After Pearl Harbor. That's in December. I think it was 1941. They made a movie about it."

I shook my head. "Wrong war."

"The Americans will let us all die," someone shouted. "They're not being bombed to Kingdom Come by Zeppelins, so why should they care?"

I looked around, trying not to panic.

"Tell them, lads," the man who had carried me to the stage shouted.

Then from beyond the railing, "What's the matter? Cat got your tongue?"

The crowd began laughing and booing; I felt the blood drain from my face.

In front of me, a scuffle broke out. One of the men who had carried us to the bandstand ripped a petition away from a man standing next to him. There was a struggle to retrieve it. The man held it up, out of reach. I leaned over the railing and tore it out of his hand. Ignoring the shouts and laughter, I scanned it. As I had hoped, there was a date at the top. August the 25th 1916. The war had over two years to go. But when did America get involved?

"America will join the war," I shouted, struggling to be heard over the roar. "You just need to be patient."

"Easy to be patient when you don't have bombs raining down on you, isn't it lad?"

More laughing and shouting.

"The mood is changing in America," I said. "There is a growing movement. We will come, I promise. You just have to hold on for a little longer."

"Don't listen to him," a woman holding a petition shouted. "The cowardly Americans will never help us."

Around her, the crowd roared their approval while others booed and called her a coward.

Charlie and I began to back away, but the men who had carried us pushed us forward. Then I heard a commotion and saw that the purple ribbon brigade was fighting their way onto the bandstand. And the red-haired girl was with them.

"We have a right to speak," the lead woman said, pushing a man out of her way.

"So do these lads," one of the other men said.

"Terrorists," someone from the crowd called. "You're trying to bring the Government down."

"We are not terrorists," the woman said, leading her group onto the bandstand. "It's the likes of you who wish to destroy our country. We are helping the war effort."

"Anarchists," someone shouted. "No votes for anarchists."

"Votes for women," the purple-ribbon ladies shouted in unison.

"And America will enter the war," I said. "Trust me."

The booing and shouting became confusing. Some women were shouting, "No votes for women," along with many of the men, but others, and some men, were cheering the women, while other people were shouting "Cowards," though at me, or the women, or the skinny guy with the petition, I couldn't tell.

Then Charlie leaned close. "Promises aren't going to work. Try something else."

"Like what?"

"I don't know, but give me the petition. I have an idea."

Chapter 8

Charlie

I held the petition high above my head. Behind me, the women were shouting at the crowd and the crowd was shouting back at them. The phrases, "Votes for women," and "Terrorists," flew back and forth. Other people were chanting, "No more war," and those surrounding them were calling them cowards, and the guy on the ground in front of me was yelling for me to give his petition back.

"Listen to me," I said.

No one did.

"Hey! Listen, I've got something to say."

Same result.

"Will you shut the hell up for one minute," I shouted.

That worked.

"Watch your language," one of the women behind me said. But some of the people in front of me were shocked into silence. It didn't lower the volume a lot, but it was enough.

"America will join the war," I said. "But it won't be for a while."

The booing started again. I took a breath, hoping I could get a few words in before they drowned me out.

"So, I think you should sign the petition. All of

you."

The people near the bandstand who could hear, looked at me in stunned silence.

From behind, one of the men who had dragged us onto the bandstand shouted, "What did you say?"

"You're right to want to leave the war," I said. "You've been fighting all alone for a long time."

"The French are fighting too," Mitch said.

"Shh," I told him, "I'm on a roll."

"No one is going to blame you if you walk away now."

One of the men came up behind me and grabbed my arm.

"What do you think you're doing?" he asked, shaking me.

I wrenched my arm away. "Reverse psychology."

"Are you calling us cowards," someone in the crowd yelled.

"No," I said. "You've put up a good fight, but you've done enough. They're dropping bombs on you. No one can stand up to that. It's only right that you quit before things get too rough."

"What's your meaning?" a woman holding one of the petitions asked. "Do you think we haven't the stomach for the fight?"

"We don't quit," someone next to her called, "we're British."

"But you're signing the petition," I said. "That means you want to quit."

"They're not quitting," the man behind me said, "they're running, with their tails between their legs."

The woman who had been gathering signatures tore up her petition and threw the pieces into the air. "We're not cowards. We're built of sterner stuff. The

46

German's don't frighten me."

Others cheered her on. More torn petitions flew into the air like confetti.

"You fools," the skinny man shouted. "Don't you see what he's doing?"

The crowd had turned, but only a little. Cries of, "No more war!" erupted while others tried to shout them down, and underneath it all, groups of people were still arguing about votes for women. There was booing, cheering, shouting, petitions being signed, and petitions being ripped up, and no one appeared to be on the same side as anyone else.

I didn't see who threw the first punch, but as soon as it happened, the whole Carfax erupted into a riot.

Me and Mitch stared in disbelief, but only for a second because the people in the crowd who weren't busy punching each other came after us. At first, they tried rushing up the stairs, but the women fought them off. Then the skinny man, and the men who had been holding him, began attacking the women from behind. There was a lot of punching and swearing and the ladies seemed to be holding their own, but then people from the crowd began climbing over the railing onto the bandstand.

I told Mitch to run, but we were surrounded and had nowhere to go. We were crushed into the group of women, fighting back-to-back in a way that reminded me of the Battle of Hastings. Unlike the Battle of Hastings, however, I didn't think Malcolm or Mendel or Mr. Merwyn or whatever the old Druid was calling himself these days, was going to ride in and save us. Then I heard the high-pitched shriek of a whistle, followed by several others. They were coming from every direction, and they were getting closer.

"Coppers," someone shouted, and suddenly people began screaming and running and the next thing I knew, we were alone—the men, the women, the skinny man with the petition, the people who had been climbing onto the bandstand to get us, were all gone. We ran to the railing and vaulted over it into the crowd. Panicked people rushed everywhere while the police shouted "Halt," and waded into the mob with their billy-clubs held high.

We tried going back the way we had come but it was blocked, so we ran the other way, and bumped into the skinny man. He grabbed us each by an arm, grinning like a cat about to pounce on a mouse.

"Help," he shouted, as we struggled against his grip. "I have the miscreants who started the riot. Over here, officers."

I was surprised at how strong he was for such a skinny guy. I couldn't break his grip, so I tried to kick him, but he slammed me and Mitch together, practically knocking the wind out of me.

"Once the police get hold of you," he hissed, "they'll see to it that you rot in jail for a very long time."

I saw two policemen struggling through the crowd trying to get to us. I twisted and pulled but couldn't break the man's grip. Then one of the purple-ribbon women came up behind the skinny man and hit him over the head with her pocketbook. I don't know what she had in it, but he dropped like an empty sack.

"You two, stop right there."

We decided not to, and ran into the crowd. A lot of other people had the same idea and, even as they continued fighting, they ran along with us. We dodged kicks and ducked fists as we tried to keep up with the stampede instead of having it trample over us. When we finally broke away, we raced across the Carfax, thinking we were finally safe. Then a whistle sounded behind us.

"Halt!"

We turned down the next street and ran, with the two policemen behind us. We had a good lead, but they had the advantage; we needed to dodge around people while the cops just shouted and everyone dove out of their way. When I glanced over my shoulder, they were almost on us.

"This way," Mitch said.

We ran into a shop. Women in long dresses, wearing hats and gloves, screamed as we ran in. We saw a door to another room behind a counter where a younger woman stood, also screaming. We ran past her and went through the door, slamming it behind us as heavy footsteps pounded into the shop. There was another door leading to the outside. I threw the latch and yanked it open and was about to run through when Mitch grabbed me and pulled me aside.

"No. They'll catch us. Here."

He pulled me behind a rack of material, and we ducked down as the cops barged in. Seeing the open door, they rushed outside.

"That's not going to fool them for very long," I said.

Mitch jumped up and ran to the door. "Long enough," he said, slamming it shut and throwing the bolt.

Seconds later, the cops were banging on it and shouting.

We ran from the room and passed the screaming women as we barged through the shop and back to the street, where we tried to blend into the crowd by walking instead of running. It seemed to work. No one looked at us, and the cops were nowhere to be seen, so we kept walking and tried not to look over our shoulders, or start running again, or anything else that would look suspicious.

We kept going and soon passed under a railway bridge.

"I think I know where we are," I said, pointing to a sign reading, Queen Street. "This train track wasn't here on our last visit, but this is where John brought us. His Aunt Esther and Cousin Maggie lived around here."

Mitch looked at the railway bridge and the Queen Street sign. "Yeah, I think you're right, but Esther was evicted, remember? And besides, that was over sixty years ago."

I sighed. "Well, it was a thought. So, what are we going to do?"

"I don't know, but I think we should get away from people for a while. We're strangers, we don't have any money, and I don't want to add to the number of people who are after us."

That sounded like a good idea, so we followed the railroad tracks until we came to open land. There we sat in a ditch, hidden from the nearby houses and anyone looking from the windows of the trains that chugged by every now and again. Visible in the distance was a church steeple and, although neither of us said anything, I'm sure we both knew that it marked the location of the footbridge over the Arun River, and the path leading to Pendragon's house.

We sat for a long time, saying nothing, and trying hard not to look at the steeple. As the hours crawled by, I grew hungry, and thirsty, and tired. In the late afternoon, a light rain began to fall, and as dusk began to draw in, I was about as miserable as I could be.

"You know," Mitch said, "we could."

I nodded. "We might as well. It probably won't amount to much. Last time we went there it was a hump in the ground."

"At least it will get us moving," he said, getting up. "I'm stiff and cold and maybe the walk will help me forget how hungry I am."

We headed across the field and walked through someone's back yard, not caring if anyone saw us, to get to the road that led to the church. From there, we took the path to the footbridge and walked along the river to where Pendragon's house used to be.

Unlike other trips, the path was smooth and firm, and when we got to the place that had been nothing but a tangle of weeds in 1851, we found a stone cottage surrounded by a neat lawn.

Mitch stopped and stared. "It looks like someone rebuilt it."

"There could be trouble inside," I said, looking at the glow from the window. "We don't know who's in there."

"Well, there's only one way to find out."

We entered the yard and walked along the flagstone path that led to the front door. Mitch took a deep breath, then knocked.

A few seconds later, the door opened. Standing in front of us was the red-haired girl, wearing a plain dress and no hat. She gaped at Mitch.

"You!"

Mitch gaped back at her. "You?"

She started to slam the door, but a hand grasped it,

stopping her. Then the girl moved aside as the door opened fully and an old woman stepped into view. She was short, hardly taller than the red-haired girl, and her white hair shone like a halo. Her face was wrinkled but not care-worn and, unlike the girl, she smiled at us.

"Mitch. Charlie. I've been expecting you. Please, come inside."

Mitch stepped across the threshold ahead of me, passing the red-haired girl, whose mouth had dropped open again.

Chapter 9

Mitch

I stepped inside, past the red-haired girl, too shocked to say anything.

"You look tired and wet," the old woman said, as she closed and latched the door. "And I bet you're hungry. Come into the parlour for some hot tea."

I looked to one side, through a wide door that led to a kitchen, much like the Shaw's, but with a large table, and the scent of fresh-baked bread wafting from it. My stomach silently begged her to take us that way but, instead, she ushered us deeper into the room, which was warmed by a crackling fire and lit by an electric lamp. A puffy sofa stood against the far wall, with a matching upholstered chair, and several wooden chairs with wicker seats, nearby. Next to them was an upright piano, a coffee table, and an end table, upon which a lamp, with an ornate, tasselled shade, rested. The woman guided us to the sofa, then turned back to the girl, who was still by the door.

"Annie, don't just stand there with your mouth hanging open, put the kettle on, and bring out some bread and jam."

I offered to sit on one of the wicker seats because my clothes were damp, but the woman told me not to be silly and insisted we both sit on the sofa, while she settled herself in the large chair. After sitting for so long in the cold and damp, it felt like heaven.

"I was starting to worry," the woman said. "When I heard about the riot in the Carfax, and Annie told me about the two young men she had met there, and that they were the ones who had saved Edith and her baby last night, I was sure it was you. I assumed you would come here straight away, and when you didn't, I feared the worst. I was about to go contact the police to see if you'd been arrested. I know how trouble seems to find you."

I looked at Charlie. He rolled his eyes and shook his head.

A sudden clatter startled me, and I looked to where the girl, Annie, had set a tray down—harder than she needed to—on the coffee table. On it were cups and saucers, a jar of jam, and a plate with a loaf of homemade bread.

"Here," she said, and sat in one of the wicker chairs.

"You've met my granddaughter, Annie—"

"Cousin," Annie said. "First cousin twice removed if we're being exact."

The woman chuckled. "She does like to remind me of that. But she spends so much time with me, she feels like my granddaughter, so that's what she is as far as I'm concerned."

I looked at Annie.

"My family are military people," she said. "They travel a lot." Then her eyes narrowed. "Why am I explaining myself to you? Who are you, anyway?"

The woman answered before I could.

"Mitch and Charlie Wyman. They're kin."

Charlie turned toward the woman. "Who are you?"

"Don't tell me you've forgot," the woman said.

54

Then she smiled. "I can't have changed that much."

Charlie leaned forward, studying her face.

"Maggie?"

The woman clapped her hands together.

"Oh, you do remember."

"It's your eyes," Charlie said. "I recognize them, from when I—"

"Told me to not be afraid to believe."

"What is going on?" Annie asked.

"These are the lads I've told you about, the ones who took my cousin John on his adventures."

Annie shook her head. "But they were just stories."

"True stories," Maggie said.

"They can't be. That was—"

"Sixty-five years ago," Charlie said, still looking at Maggie. "I can't believe it's really you. You were eight years old."

"But you," Annie said, glaring at me and Charlie, "you're barely more than boys. Are you going to try to convince me you're a hundred years old?"

"We're seventeen," Charlie said. "We were sixteen when we first met Maggie."

"And how—"

"Time moves differently where we're from."

"I wasn't going to ask how it worked," Annie said, "I was going to ask how you expected me to believe that."

"Because they are sitting in front of you," Maggie said. "And they are the same lads I met when I was eight. They are the cloak bearers, the Guardians of the Talisman. The travellers I told you about when you were a little girl."

"The knights?" Annie asked. "They certainly don't

look like knights."

"Knights don't always wear armour and ride white horses," Maggie said.

"And vagrants don't fly through time like in an H. G. Wells novel."

"We're not vagrants," Charlie said.

"Well, if you are the cloak bearers," Annie asked, "where's your cloak?"

"We left it with Edith," I said.

"Then go get it."

"We can't," Charlie said.

"The Shaw's, um, Mr. Shaw, actually," I said. "He's not someone we want to run into."

"Thought so," Annie said, as if that settled the argument.

"But it's true," Charlie said. "He wants to set the law on us."

"You do attract trouble, don't you?" Maggie said, smiling at Charlie.

Annie smirked. "So, you've no proof at all."

I thought about agreeing with her, then I had an idea.

"I can show you something better than the cloak," I said, looking at Maggie. "That table in the kitchen, where did you get it?"

Maggie gazed toward the kitchen. "When my mother bought this land, the men she hired to clear it found a slab of oak, miraculously preserved in the clay. They said it could be hundreds of years old. So, we sent it to a craftsman who made it into a table for us."

"It's more like two thousand years old," I said, "and we've seen it many times. It was originally the door to the house that later became Pendragon's home. At that time, his family were using it as a table, and that was when I made a carving in it. It should still be there."

"That's insane," Annie said.

"But will it convince you?"

Annie eyed me coolly. "You're bluffing. You're just hoping there's a random scar on the table that you can claim as proof."

I was going to say it was a carving of an airliner, but decided that wasn't such a good idea. "It's a cross," I said. "And there's a knot in the middle of it."

"In all the years I've sat at that table," Annie said, "I have seen no such thing."

"Nor have I," Maggie said. "But let's go look for it."

She rose, picked up the tray with the untouched loaf of bread on it, and went toward the kitchen. I looked at Charlie, who shrugged, and Annie, who rolled her eyes, then followed Maggie.

The kitchen was lit by an electric light suspended from the ceiling above the table. Maggie put the tray on a counter, then reached for a copper kettle that was sitting on top of the black stove.

"That was never going to boil," she said, resting her hand against the kettle. "I don't know what's wrong with that girl."

She opened a door on the stove and used a poker to stir up the embers within. Soon a flame started, and she closed the door. "There," she said, "now let's have a look for that carving."

Charlie entered the kitchen, followed by Annie, and the four of us cleared the dishes off the table and removed the white tablecloth.

"There you go, time-traveling boy," Annie said,

"find the carving."

I looked at one end of the table, then the other, and soon found the dark knot I was looking for, but the carving wasn't there. I began to fear that the craftsman might have sanded it out, but then I took a closer look.

"Something wrong, sir knight?" Annie asked. "Your carving not there?"

She had come to stand next to me, and looked at the knot I had pointed to, a smirk on her face. I turned to her and smiled. "It's on the other side."

The table was so heavy it took the four of us to turn it over. When it finally lay on the floor, it's legs in the air, I looked at the other side of the knot. The carving, though faded with age, was clearly visible.

"Well, I'll be," Maggie said, leaning close.

Annie said nothing, but her mouth was hanging open again.

◆

By the time we got the table back in place, the kettle was boiling. Maggie filled a teapot, and we were finally able to drink some tea and eat the bread and jam, which was delicious, while she and Annie prepared a meal. Annie, however, remained unconvinced.

"Your story still sounds impossible," she said. "And random marks on the underside of the table aside, you can't expect me to believe the impossible."

I nodded. "That's fair enough. We can hardly believe it ourselves, and it's happening to us. Besides, you don't really need to believe we've been here before. You only need to believe we're here now."

"That's right," Maggie said, setting a steaming pot on the table. "No matter how they got here, you can't deny what's in front of you. Don't fret about the rest of it, just accept what your eyes can see."

Annie sat across the table from us, her arms folded, her brow furrowed. "You are certainly here," she said. "I can't deny that. But it doesn't make the rest of their story true."

Maggie ignored her.

"I suspected it was you when I first heard about the bombing," she said, ladling stew onto our plates. "That house was built right over the spot where you appeared last time."

"How do you know where we appeared?" Charlie asked.

Annie's fork clinked on her plate as she dropped it. "What do you mean, appeared?"

"John showed me," Maggie said, looking at Charlie.

"You've seen John?"

"Certainly. He's been to visit several times over the years. He's got children, and grandchildren. I've met them, as well."

I looked at her. "Got, not had? Is he still alive?"

Maggie sat, spooning stew onto her own plate. "Oh, yes. Turned eighty this year, he did, but he's still spry as a spring rabbit. He owns a farm up north, near Clithero. Bought it with the reward money."

"That's right," Charlie said. "We got money last time we were here." He looked at Maggie. "That's how you bought this house, isn't it? With the money we gave you."

Maggie nodded, smiling. "Mother did, but yes, it is thanks to you that we are all here enjoying this meal."

"Money?" Annie asked.

"Yes," Charlie said. "We each got a hundred pounds from Queen Victoria—"

"Prince Albert, actually," I said, looking at Annie. "He had to talk her into it."

Annie fumbled for her fork. "This is insane."

I looked away. "Yes. Maybe we should talk about something else."

"Like why you're here," Maggie said. "John told me he figured out why you had come last time."

"They must be here to go fight in France," Annie said.

Charlie shook his head. "I really hope not."

"We haven't had time," I said. "And so far, we haven't a clue."

Maggie picked up a big knife and began cutting slices of bread. "Did you bring anything with you? Like last time?"

Charlie dug the bullet out of his pocket and held it up. "Just this."

"So, you must be meant to fight," Annie said.

"Why are you so eager to send us to war?" I asked, becoming annoyed.

"Because that's what men, brave men, do."

"What is it," Maggie asked.

"Dunno" Charlie said. "A bullet of some kind."

"But not like any I've ever seen," I said.

Maggie shook her head. "It's not for a hunting rifle. That's for certain. It looks military."

"Please don't say you think it means we need to go fight," Charlie said.

"Hold on," Annie said, leaning across the table. "Let me see that." She snatched it out of Charlie's hand and sat back.

"Hey! Give that back."

Annie ignored him. "It's a three-oh-three machine gun bullet," she said, rolling it in her fingers and bouncing it on her palm. "It's not live. So why …" She twisted the bullet and pulled the pointed copper shell from the casing. "Thought so," she said, sniffing the base of the bullet. Then she held it out so we could see. "Explain this."

The bullet had been hollowed out and packed with a yellow-grey substance.

"I don't—"

"It's a Buckingham bullet," she said, her voice rising. "Where did you get it?"

"Our grandfather sent it to us."

"So, where did he get it? How could he have access to one? Where does he live?"

I felt like saying, "He lives in 2018," but I didn't think that would help. I ended up saying nothing because Annie filled the silence.

"This is an incendiary bullet," Annie said, her voice still louder than it needed to be. "Only those people who need to know about these should have one."

"Incendiary?" Charlie asked.

"It burns when it's fired," Annie said. "And it's top secret. It's being developed in secret military laboratories, and they are only available to special airmen. You couldn't have been sent this, unless your grandfather works in the High Command, or is a spy."

She spit the final words at us, her face turning red.

"It's a tracer bullet?" I asked.

Charlie smirked and shook his head. "If it's so top secret, how do you know about it?"

Annie sat back. "I … I can't tell you."

"So, you're the spy," Charlie said. "Maybe we're here to expose you."

Maggie clapped her hands. "I think we're getting off track. You've come with that bullet, so there must be a reason, and Annie, you seem to know something about it, so you'd best tell us."

Annie turned red. "I'm not supposed to. It's classified."

"This is to do with Uncle Henry, isn't it?"

Annie nodded. I looked at Maggie. "Uncle Henry?"

"My late husband's sister's nephew-in-law," she said. "Apparently, he's based around here."

"It's a secret base," Annie said. "Where they're experimenting with these types of bullets. Making them better. To use against the Zeppelins. It's critical work. And top secret. And we're not supposed to talk about it."

"If it's secret," I asked, "then how do you know about it."

Annie's eyes narrowed. "Because he took me there."

"And why—"

"Because he knows about my dedication to woman's rights. He respects my intelligence. He knows I can be trusted with important information."

"Or," Maggie said, giving Annie a sly smile, "he was attempting to impress a pretty, young girl."

Annie flushed. "He's my uncle."

"Well, you can't be that trustworthy," Charlie said. "You've just spilled the beans to us."

Annie turned a deeper shade of red, but not from embarrassment this time. Maggie clapped her hands again.

"That must be it, then," she said. "You've got that bullet. Annie can contact Henry. It's obvious."

"Not to me," Charlie said.

"We can't just show up at a secret base," Annie said. And for once, I agreed with her.

Maggie picked up a slice of bread and began slowly buttering it. "You're clever, all of you. You'll think of something."

Chapter 10
Saturday, 26 August 1916

Charlie

We left early the next morning, after a long night of making plans. We talked through dinner, then while we helped clear up, and then while sitting at the big table, drinking endless cups of tea long into the night.

In the end, we decided to keep as close to the truth as we could. Me and Mitch were Americans, sent to England with an advanced incendiary bullet to deliver to the British military. It was critical, because the American Government wanted Britain to win the war, and it was top secret because the American people didn't want to get involved. We were chosen, not because we were secret agents or anything, but because we were related to Annie, and Military Intelligence knew she could help us contact her Uncle Henry. We had that part down solid, but the rest was a little fuzzy. I didn't have a good feeling about it, but everyone was tired, so Maggie made up two extra beds and we settled in for a short sleep.

In the morning, after an early breakfast, Maggie gave us money for the train, and me and Mitch a little extra because she felt she owed us. We didn't object; we didn't know how long we'd be stuck there, and money always comes in handy.

Annie came with us, naturally. She was the only one who knew how to find the base, and without her, we'd probably end up in trouble again. Navigating the past is difficult, and there always seems to be someone around eager to throw us in jail, or worse. So, Annie took us to the station, helped us buy tickets and, when the train pulled in, told us where to get on and where to sit.

The trains had improved since our previous visit, having larger engines, more comfortable carriages, and individual compartments. And that's where Annie had us sit, in a side room off a narrow hallway that we accessed through a sliding door. I sat on one of the bench seats, with Mitch and Annie across from me. It was small, but private; ideal for continuing our discussion.

I expected, since the inside of the train was comfortable, that the ride would be smooth. But as I was about to pick up the conversation from the night before, the train lurched forward, throwing me against the wall, and Annie against Mitch. He had to grab her to keep her from falling on the floor, and she squealed with surprised laughter. As the train shuddered and clattered over the rails, they settled back into the seat, sitting just a little closer together than they had been.

"What happens when we get to the base?" I asked. "Who's going to be in charge?"

"In cars?" Mitch said. At least I think he did. The clatter and hiss of the engine came in through the compartment's half open window, along with smoke and soot, making it both hard to hear and difficult to breathe.

Bracing myself against the rolling of the carriage, I

tried to close the window. It wouldn't budge, so I flopped back into my seat. Then the door slid open and a man wearing a suit and carrying a newspaper stepped inside. He slammed the window closed, sat on the seat next to me and began reading.

I looked at the man's paper and saw the headline: "Local Woman in Narrow Escape as Zeppelin Rains Fire on Horsham." Below it was a photo of the bombed house, and beneath that another article titled: "Where Are the Angels?" with the subheading: "Woman Claims Angels Saved Her: Are They the Same Men Who Started the Riot in the Carfax?" I scanned the first paragraph as best I could on the bumpy train, and read that "the two men, with American accents and distinctive ginger hair, disappeared from the scene, then reappeared in the Carfax the following morning. Anyone with information …"

I looked away so the man couldn't see my face. When I caught Mitch's eye, I nodded toward the newspaper. He read the headline, then whispered in Annie's ear. After she got a look at the paper, she put a finger to her lips, leaned up against Mitch and pretended to sleep. So, Mitch leaned against the wall and closed his eyes. I did the same, and the three of us kept still and silent until we got to Earlswood, which was where we needed to get off because that was the closest town to the base.

We stepped out of the station and onto a busy street, with a cluster of horse-drawn cabs, and even some cars, waiting near the entrance.

"The base isn't far," Annie said, walking past the cabs. "It's only about five miles outside of town."

"Hey," I called, pointing to the cabs. "What are

they for?"

Annie gave them a quick look. "Other people."

"We've got money. We could—"

"And if you walk, you'll still have it at the end of your journey."

To my surprise, Mitch joined her. "She's right," he said, striding after her.

And so, we walked.

I wasn't happy about it, but after a while I had to agree that it was more pleasant and would give us a chance to talk. The sun was shining, the air was comfortably cool, and the road wasn't as rutted and muddy as some of the ones we had been forced to march on. Agreeing on what we were going to do once we got to the base, however, didn't seem to be in the cards. Mitch and Annie walked ahead, strolling as if they were in a country park, their heads together, chatting about nothing instead of making plans. She was encouraging Mitch to tell her what he thought about women voting, and he was trying to steer the conversation to our more impressive exploits.

I heard him giving his opinions about equality and how women were as capable as men, while Annie gushed, and then he started telling her about the time we had marched with Harold's army all the way from London to York. She listened politely and didn't scoff, which was a huge improvement over her reactions the night before. I noticed, however, that he neglected to tell her about how we had collapsed from exhaustion and would have died if the old Druid hadn't helped us. I'm sure he left the Druid part out because he was trying to impress her, but I still thought it was a good move; she might be willing to go along with a story about Harold, but an immortal

Druid and a magic stone called the Talisman might be too much.

It got me thinking about them, however. My hope was, once we got to the base, that the Druid would be there to greet us. That was the only way I could see this working. Despite what Annie had said about her uncle, I couldn't see him welcoming us onto his base, and I think she knew that. And I think that was why she was oohing and aahing over Mitch's stories rather than trying to work out what we were going to do once we got there.

Because Annie was paying more attention to Mitch—coupled with the fact that she had only been there once, and it was, after all, a secret base—we went wrong a few times. But near midday, after turning down a side road that looked as if it had more traffic than you might expect, I felt certain we were going the right way. This was confirmed a few minutes later when, not far ahead, I saw a gate, festooned with barbed wire, and flanked by two sentries pointing rifles at us.

"Halt!" one of them said. "Go back the way you came. This is a restricted area."

We all stopped, then Annie took a few steps forward.

"My name is Annie McAllister. Major Henry Billings is my uncle. We need to see him. I have something very important to show him. He will want to see us."

"Yer daft, the lot of ya," the other soldier said, raising his rifle higher and taking aim at Annie. "Away now."

Annie stood firm. "I demand to see my uncle."

The soldier kept her in his sight. "And I demand

you leave. Now."

"But we need—"

"You need to decide what your future is going to look like," the soldier said. "Option one is, you turn around and go back the way you came, and we all get to enjoy the day. Option two is, I call the local constabulary and turn you over to them. And they take a dim view of civilians meddling in military business. Or you can choose option three, which is me shooting you where you stand and getting a medal for my efforts. Now, what is it going to be?"

The other soldier now aimed at Mitch. Annie's shoulders slumped. We had banked everything on her being able to get us onto the base, and we didn't have a back-up plan. In the seconds of silence that followed, I realized our entire plan had been terminally flawed. Uncle Henry wasn't going to see Annie. He might be her uncle, and he might have acted like family when he took her on a tour of the base, but first and foremost he was the commander of a military base. A family connection wasn't going to convince them, but a military connection might.

I stepped around Annie and Mitch and stared at the two guards pointing their rifles at me. I had never been in the military, but I had been conscripted enough times to know what motivated them.

"Soldier," I shouted, standing as straight as I could. "Lower that weapon and take us to your commanding officer."

"Says you?"

I put my fists on my hips and glared at them. "Yes. Says me." The rifles lowered, just a little.

I kept my eyes on them. "Now I'm giving you some options. One: you take us to Major Billings, and if we are not who we say we are, you can lock us up."

The soldier shook his head. "I am not disturbing the commanding officer on your say so."

"Two," I said, ignoring him. "You send us away. But we will return, and at some point, we will get to see Major Billings. And then you will have to explain why our important mission is behind schedule."

"You're a Yank," the first soldier said, bringing his rifle back up.

"I'm an ally," I said. "Now choose your option. If we walk away without seeing Major Billings, you will both have a great deal of explaining to do. Now which is it?"

The two soldiers looked at each other.

"What are Americans doing here?"

"I don't know."

"And the girl? Is she really the Major's niece?"

"I don't know?"

They said nothing for a while, each one afraid to make a decision. I watched them, my arms folded, waiting. Then I said, "Before we leave, I want your names so I can report to Major Billings who stopped us from seeing him."

"I'll not give you—"

"That's fine," I said, turning away. "There will be a roster."

"Alright, alright," he said. "All of you, come this way."

With both rifles trained on us, we approached the gate.

"Hands behind your heads," he shouted as we got near, "and eyes on the ground. Walk."

He left the other guard at the gate and followed us, no doubt keeping his rifle trained on Mitch's back the whole time, playing a hostile game of Blind Man's Bluff with us.

"Forward," he shouted. "Turn right. Stop. Left face. Walk. Stop here."

With my head down, I could see only that we were standing on a slab of concrete next to a building, and there was a door in front of us. The door opened. A pair of army boots came into view.

"What is the meaning of this?"

"Three civilians to see Major Billings."

"Just one civilian," I said. "The Major's niece."

"Shut it."

"Major Billings will have my head if I bring them in."

"Your choice," the soldier said, already moving away.

"Corporal Rawlins, get back here."

"I am required at the gate for guard duty," the soldier, now even further away, replied.

I lifted my head. The soldier at the door was a shade shorter than me, with light brown hair, and sergeant stripes on his sleeve.

"Sergeant," I said, "we request to see Major Billings."

"On whose authority?"

"That is for the Major's ears only."

"Who are you? And why is she with you?"

"That will all become clear when we see Major Billings."

The soldier sighed. "Come in, then."

We stepped into a small room containing a wooden file cabinet, a desk with a typewriter and a mass of papers covering it, and a small table with an antique telephone on it. Aside from that, there was only a window and a second door. The soldier tapped on it with his knuckle.

"What is it, Sergeant Dobson?" The voice from beyond the door was gruff and impatient.

Dobson cleared his throat. "Pardon me for the intrusion, Major, but you have visitors."

"Visitors?" the Major bellowed. "We don't have visitors here. Send them away."

"One claims to be your niece, sir."

A few seconds of silence followed. Then the Major, his voice restrained, said, "Send them in."

If Annie was expecting her uncle to greet her with open arms, she was badly mistaken.

"What do you think you're playing at, young lady?" he shouted as soon as the three of us lined up in front of his desk. He was a short, heavyset man with a balding head and round, wire-rimmed glasses, which made him look more like a college professor than an Army Major. He didn't bother to stand up to berate us, but even sitting down, his voice cut to the bone. "Bringing your friends to a military base? You silly, little girl. I should have the lot of you thrown into the glasshouse."

At that point, Annie started sniffling and Mitch looked like he wanted to comfort her, and that wouldn't have done us any good. I took a breath, stood at attention, and continued the charade.

"Permission to speak, sir."

The Major stopped shouting and glared at me. "Who—"

"Sergeant Charles Wyman, United States Army. I am here with Corporal Mitchell Wyman, United States Army, on a sensitive mission."

The Major sat back. "You'd better not be having a

72

laugh, son, because I am—"

I took the bullet out of my pocket and placed it on the desk in front of him. Billings looked at the bullet, then back at me.

"What is this?"

"What you call a Buckingham Bullet, sir. It's an incendiary round, using the most advanced formula devised by the US military."

At least I hoped it did. The bullet was old, but not a hundred years old, so whatever sort of powder it used, it was likely to be better than anything they had come up with. Billings picked up the bullet, pulled it apart and looked at the base of the slug.

"Where did you get this?"

"The United States Army, sir."

Billings said nothing for a while. He looked at me, and Mitch, who was also, thankfully, standing at attention, and then back at the bullet.

"Dobson," he barked, after a minute or two.

"Sir?" Dobson said, opening the door suspiciously soon after his summons.

"Take this to Captain Jeffreys," Billings said, holding up the bullet.

Dobson took the bullet and left.

When we heard the outer door close, Billings leaned back in his chair. "Now suppose you tell me what this is all about, young man."

Here, at least, our planning came in handy. I told him the story we had concocted but linked it to the US army. I kept the story as concise as I could, hoping brevity would keep me from exposing its cracks.

"So, you are involved in the research and manufacture of these bullets?" Billings asked when I finished.

"No, sir. Me and my brother are regular army. We were recruited because we are related to Miss McAllister, and it was surmised that she could gain us access to you."

Billings picked up a pencil and tapped it against the desktop. "And how does the US Army know about this base, and my relation to Miss McAllister?"

"This mission is top secret," I said. "We were recruited on a need-to-know basis. And we do not need to know that."

"Convenient," Billings said. "And how did you get over here? Surely you know that."

"Indeed, sir, but that's confidential."

Billings laid the pencil down and nodded. "Of course it is." Once again, he looked from me to Mitch, his brow furrowed. "Your story sounds like a fairytale. And it smells like—"

A pounding of footsteps and a knock at the door made him stop.

"What now?"

The door opened and Sergeant Dobson entered, breathing hard. "Captain Jefferys, sir. He wants you at the lab."

Chapter 11

Mitch

"Thank you, Sergeant," Uncle Henry said. "Tell him I'll be along as soon as I am finished here."

Dobson looked uncertain. "He said it was urgent, sir." Then he nodded at me and Charlie. "And he wants to see them as well."

Henry sighed and heaved himself out of his chair. "Very well," he said, striding across the office. "You two, with me. Annie, stay here. Dobson, remain in the outer office and make sure she does not leave.

"Am I a prisoner now?" Annie asked.

Henry, nearly at the door, spun around to face her. "Watch your tongue, young lady. This is a military base. Civilians are not meant to be here. As for prison, you have done enough already to merit the confines of a cell for many years, but out of respect for your mother, I am willing to overlook your transgressions. Now, for your own safety, you will remain here until we return. Is that clear?"

Annie, practically glowing crimson, nodded. I felt bad for her, but there was nothing I could do. Charlie had told Henry we were soldiers, so I had to act like one, even though he annoyingly made himself outrank me.

Henry turned back to the door and glared at Dobson. "Are your duties clear, sergeant?"

"Yes, sir," Dobson said, saluting.

After we left the building, Henry shook his head. "I don't know what's going on here, but as soon as I find out what Captain Jeffreys wants, I will decide what to do with you two. And, unlike my niece, I do not have a soft spot for you."

He glared at me, as if expecting an answer.

"No, sir," I said.

Henry nodded. "This way. Follow me."

My head was spinning and, once again, the prospect of prison hung over us, but it was my first chance to see the base properly, so I took a good look around. It was small, and consisted mostly of a large, flat field and a scattering of buildings. There were several sentries patrolling the high, barbed wire fence, and other soldiers nearby trying to look busy. Henry led us across the field, toward a long, low structure on the far side of the base, well away from the other buildings. It was easily the largest building there, larger even than the barn-sized shed we were walking past. The shed's large doors were open and inside I saw two airplanes. They were tiny and looked like they were made of tissue paper and wires and they each had two wings—an upper and a lower—instead of just one. They must have been models and not actual airplanes because no one would be crazy enough to fly in something like that.

The building we were heading for, Henry told us, was the lab, and it looked like it had been built recently and in a hurry. It was made of rough, unpainted boards topped with a tin roof, and it ran along one side of the base near the perimeter fence. There was a single door at one end, and only a few windows spaced along its length, all covered with shutters. Despite this, the interior—I discovered as Henry ushered us inside—was bright, thanks to the numerous electric lights suspended from the ceiling. The single, long room was filled with work benches, shelves, and several strange-looking machines. At the nearest workbench, a man about my height, with brown hair and thick glasses was bent over a metal plate, stirring a small mound of grey powder with a glass rod. Behind the metal plate was a rack of test tubes, each containing different coloured powders. Next to the rack was our bullet.

"Jeffreys, what is so urgent that you call me away—"

Jeffreys stopped stirring and, ignoring Henry, looked at me and Charlie. "Where did you get that bullet?"

Charlie repeated, a little more succinctly, the story about us being on a secret mission. Jeffreys beamed at him as he talked.

"We owe your country, and you, a huge debt of gratitude," Jeffreys said when Charlie finished. Then he came to us and shook our hands.

"What are you on about?" Henry asked.

Jeffreys went back to his pile of powder. "After extracting the incendiary pellet from the slug, I did an initial analysis and found it is well advanced compared to ours. I have combined some ingredients according to my findings, but I will need more time, and additional chemicals, to recreate it exactly. However, the mixture I have made using what is available will, I hope, be an improvement."

Jeffreys scooped up some of the powder with a tiny spoon and poured it on another metal plate. Then he struck a match. "Stand away," he said, and we all took a few steps back as he touched the match to the powder.

A greenish flame shot up about six inches, settled back to about half that height, and continued to burn for another second or two before dying away, leaving nothing but a black scorch-mark on the plate.

"That's amazing," Jeffreys said, still staring at the plate. Then he turned toward us. "How did the American's develop this?"

"That's not for us to know," Charlie said. "Our mission was to deliver the bullet. And it is top secret. Anything you reverse engineer from what we gave you must be presented as something you developed on your own. America cannot be known to have had a hand in this."

"Understood, Sergeant Wyman," Jeffreys—who knew Charlie's pretend rank because, of course, he had managed to mention it while telling his story—said.

"And our involvement must remain secret."

"I will happily comply," Henry said. "Solitary confinement for the duration of the war will fulfil that requirement."

I felt myself go pale.

"That would be a poor way of showing appreciation," Jeffreys said. "You saw the same thing I did, Henry. You know what this means."

Henry grunted. "I still don't like it. This formula, appearing out of nowhere, just when we—"

"Our friends the Americans gave it to us. And at this point we need all the friends we can get. Locking up these men will not encourage them to help us in the future."

Henry stepped forward, took a glass rod, and

poked at the pile of powder.

"Will this solve our problem?"

"Once we procure the necessary chemicals, I have every confidence we can achieve our objective."

Henry continued staring at the powder.

"We can't just let them go."

"But you can't put them in prison," Jeffreys said, lowering his voice. "They're American soldiers, for God's sake."

"We have not yet established—"

"What are your plans, Sergeant?" Jeffreys said, turning to Charlie.

At that moment, I was glad Charlie outranked me because my mind was blank. Fortunately, Charlie had an answer ready."

"Our mission was to deliver the bullet," Charlie said. "There was no extraction plan. We were to remain with Annie and her family and make our own way back when and as we could."

Jeffreys rubbed his chin. "That sounds rather extraordinary."

Charlie nodded. "These are extraordinary times."

"So," Henry said, "you are on extended, or shall we say, indefinite leave from the US Army?"

That didn't sound like it was good for us, but after Charlie nodded, Henry, for the first time, smiled.

"Then I believe I have a suitable solution." He looked at Jeffreys. "Your office. We need to sort this out in private."

I looked around. There were only two other people in the lab. They were far away and appeared to be working, but they did glance our way every now and again.

Henry took the bullet, put it in his pocket, and

said, "Follow."

Charlie went after him, but I hesitated, looking at the pile of powder.

"Did our bullet really help that much?" I asked.

Jeffreys put a hand on my shoulder.

"Son, what you gave us could make the difference between victory and defeat. That single bullet might just win the war."

Chapter 12

Charlie

It wasn't much of an office, just an area enclosed by two walls made of rough boards, and all it contained was a wooden file cabinet and a battered oak desk covered in papers. It was also small, so we had to stand uncomfortably close together until Major Billings stepped to the far side of the desk where, I noted, there wasn't even a chair.

The Major leaned forward, his hands flat on the desk. "Fortunately for you, locking you up will be more trouble than it's worth. Plus, it will only draw attention. Your story may be poppycock," here, he glared hard at Mitch, "but your bullet is real, and wherever it came from, it needs to remain secret. So, this is what is going to happen." He leaned closer, switching his gaze to me. "We need men, and if, as you claim, you are on indefinite leave from the US Army, that means you are free to join the British Army."

"But we're Americans, sir," I said.

The Major smiled and shook his head. "No, you're not. You're Canadian soldiers, on secondment to our little base. That will explain your accent. And sticking to your claim that you are related to my niece may help smooth over your unorthodox arrival. Let's say you were allowed a brief visit prior to reporting for duty and that your belongings were lost in transit. I'll write up the orders, Sergeant Dobson will fill in the details to make it look above board. Then you will—"

"What part?" Mitch asked.

I went pale; you are not supposed to interrupt an officer, but Major Billings merely scowled at him. "Your meaning, corporal?"

"Where in Canada are we supposed to be from. Someone is bound to ask."

The Major sighed. "Where would you like to be from?"

"Quebec," I said.

Mitch shook his head. "No, they speak French there. We need someplace obscure, and closer to home. There's a small town, in the province of Ontario, just over the border with New York, called Cornwall. There's a bridge from Rooseveltown that goes over the St. Lawrence River to Cornwall Island, in Ontario, and another leading to the town of Cornwall. If anyone becomes curious, the confusion with the English county of Cornwall will become the main talking point, allowing us to avoid being tripped up by details."

Major Billings stood straight and rubbed his chin. "Well thought, Corporal."

Unable to stop myself, I asked, "How do you know all that?"

Mitch smirked. "I saw it on a documentary."

"You'll need uniforms," Billings said, raking through the papers on the desk. He picked one up, looked at it and turned it over. Then he found a pencil and began writing. "You're big lads," he said, glancing up at us. "Height and weight, corporal."

"Uh, I'm five feet seven inches and weigh one

hundred and twenty-nine pounds," Mitch said.

Billings scribbled on the paper. "Nine stone three. Sergeant?"

"Five seven and a half. One hundred and thirty-four."

"Nine stone eight," Billings mumbled, still scribbling. He signed the bottom of the sheet with a flourish, folded it and held it out to Jeffreys. "Get this to the Quartermaster. Tell him it's urgent."

Jeffreys took the paper and left. Billings stood with his hands on his hips, giving us a stony stare. "You're mine now. You'll do what I say when I say, or I'll have you court marshalled and locked up. Is that clear?"

"Crystal," I said, as Mitch nodded.

Billings folded his arms across his chest and his look softened. "But more importantly, you now have the rare privilege of serving in the British Army. I trust you will grasp this opportunity with the appropriate amount of enthusiasm."

"Yes, sir," we said in unison.

Jeffreys returned then. Billings looked surprised.

"I found Corporal Blake outside," Jeffreys said. "He's taking the message to the Quartermaster, and he will return with the uniforms."

Billings nodded. "Excellent. Now we're together, we need to get this straight." He cleared a space in the middle of the desk, took our bullet from his pocket and set it down so it stood upright. "We four, and my niece, are the only people who know about this, am I correct."

"Well, there's Maggie," I said. "She was there when I showed it to Annie."

Billings grunted. "But no one else?"

83

"No, sir."

"Then that's how we must keep it. You said yourself that it must look as if we developed the bullet on our own, so from here on, no one must say anything about it. You are simply two Canadian soldiers serving in the British Army. That is not so unusual as to cause suspicion. You will be assigned jobs. You will do your duty quietly and competently, and above all, you will keep your heads down and draw no attention to yourselves. Is that clear?"

"Yes, sir," I said along with Mitch, wondering if he was experiencing the same sinking feeling I was.

"And Jeffreys," Billings continued. "Whatever you develop must be presented as your work alone. No one, not even Captains Farber and Newell, are to be let in on this secret. Understood?"

"Absolutely," Jeffreys said.

"How soon can we expect a prototype?"

Jeffreys gazed at the ceiling for a few seconds. "My initial analysis was encouraging. I've done all I can with what I have available. Depending on when we get the proper chemicals, I'd say no more than a day or two. And once we have a successful test, we can start production immediately."

"So, our problem could be eradicated within the week?"

Jeffreys nodded. "Depending on the chemicals."

"Then we'll get on it immediately."

That pretty much ended the meeting—with us, once again, conscripted into the army, with our cloak out of reach, and wondering how we could ever get back home. Billings and Jeffreys left us in the office while they went to his workbench to play around with chemicals. They told us to wait, so we leaned up against the desk, careful not to disturb any papers.

"What a mess," I said.

Mitch stared at the floor for a while before speaking. "I don't know. It could be worse. At least it's fairly modern, and we'll have a bed to sleep in. And, if you think about it, we've already completed our mission. There's nothing left for us to do except go back home."

I turned and looked at the bullet, still standing in the middle of the desk. "Yeah, but how are we going to work that? We still can't get to the house, and we don't have our cloak."

Mitch shrugged. "The house isn't going anywhere, and it will cool down enough in a few days for us to get back to our spot, and we know where our cloak is, we just need to convince Edith to give it back."

"Except, if Mr. Shaw sees us, he'll have us put in jail, and don't forget that we're in the army now. Major Billings owns us, and he's not going to let us out of his sight."

"Well, at some point, the Druid will show up. He always does, and he'll help put things right."

I nodded, but not enthusiastically. "That's a crap plan."

"Yeah," Mitch said, "but it's the only one we have."

We waited silently for a while, then Billings came in, holding a package wrapped in brown paper and tied with string. He handed it to me.

"Your uniforms. Put them on and wrap your old clothes up."

With that, he left. The uniforms fit surprisingly well; mine had sergeant stripes on it while Mitch's had the double chevrons of a corporal.

"How come you outrank me?" he asked, clearly put out.

"Because I came up with the plan."

"I'm older, I should outrank you."

I shrugged. "Do a good job. Maybe Major Billings will promote you."

We stepped out of the office, but when Major Billings saw us, he herded us back in.

"Here are your orders," he said, taking the package of clothing from me and shoving it at Mitch. "You, Corporal Wyman, will take this to Sergeant Dobson. You will give it to him, and to no one else, and you will not speak to my niece. You will then report to Flight Lieutenant Huntington at the hangar. Is that clear?"

"Yes sir."

Billings turned to me.

"You, Sergeant Wyman, arrived at the most opportune time. Captain Newell, in charge of Ammunition Activation for our diminutive but highly efficient and top-secret military laboratory," (which he pronounced as la-BOR-a-tory) "finds himself in urgent need of a new assistant, and you are of sufficient rank to be his replacement. Captain Jeffreys will take you to him."

"Yes sir."

Billings turned to go.

"Uh, sir?"

"Yes, Sergeant."

"The other assistant, what happened to him?"

He stopped for a moment, his back still to me. "He blew himself up."

Mitch followed Billings out of the office, turning as he left to grin at me.

Chapter 13

Mitch

I wasn't really happy that Charlie got the dangerous job. In fact, it worried me a little, but it was his own fault. I just hoped he'd be more careful than the other guy.

Henry marched on ahead of me, apparently on his way to inspect the rest of the operation, so I ducked out the door and headed back to his office. When I knocked on the door, Dobson opened it.

"So, you're pretending to be British Soldiers now?"

"No," I said, pushing past him, "we're real soldiers. Henry, I mean, Major Billings, has accepted our transfer. You'll be getting all the paperwork soon."

Dobson eyed me suspiciously. "Well, no skin off my nose. What are your orders?"

"I'm to give you this, and report to the hangar."

Dobson smiled. "Ah, Brody. I'm sure you and he will get along fine." He looked at the package. "And what's this?"

I held it out. "Our civilian clothes."

I felt someone brush by me and pull the package from my hands.

"I'll take this," Annie said, smiling at Dobson. Then she turned toward me and lowered her voice.

"You look quite smart. I like a man in uniform."

"Um, I'm not supposed to talk to you," I said. "Major Billings' orders."

Annie smiled. "We'll see about that."

"And you're to arrange transport for, ah, Miss McAllister," I said to Dobson.

"Thank you for relaying the message, corporal," he said, emphasizing the words to let me know I wasn't giving him orders. "I think you should shove off now, before the Major finds you disobeyed him and has you shot."

"Yes, Sergeant," I said, as I walked through the door.

Annie followed, carrying the package. Dobson tried to stop her.

"Miss, you can't—"

"I can and I will, sergeant."

"The Major's orders—"

"You can tattle to my uncle, the Major, if you wish, but whatever comes of it, my father, the Colonel, will sort it out. Now will you allow me to say good-by to my cousin?"

Dobson mumbled something and the next thing I knew, Annie was standing in front of me, still holding the package.

"Cousin?" I asked.

She shrugged. "I assumed we're related somehow. Cousin works, doesn't it?"

"Well, distant cousins," I said.

Her face coloured slightly. "I have a favour to ask. Can I see you tomorrow?"

I let out a short laugh. "I doubt your uncle—"

"I wasn't kidding about my father," she said, looking up at me. "Now, do you want to see me, or not?"

I nodded. "Yes, yes I do."

"Good," she said, smiling. "It's settled, then."

She started to move away.

"Wait," I said, holding her arm.

I peeled a flap of the package aside and felt for my pants. Wiggling my hand around, I found my pocket, and pulled out the feather.

"I almost forgot this," I said, holding it up.

Her shoulders slumped. "I wish you'd let me take that back."

"No way," I said, putting it in my pocket. "It brings me luck and reminds me of you."

To my surprise, she leaned in and kissed my cheek. "Tomorrow then," she said, strolling away. "And wear your uniform. You look smashing in it."

"I'll have to," I said, feeling slightly light-headed. "It's all I have."

As I made my way to the hangar, I struggled to get the smile off my face. By the time I arrived, I felt I looked appropriately sombre.

The hangar was a huge building with a flat roof and a wide-open front. The two model airplanes were inside, as were two men wearing grease-stained mechanic overalls. They were working on the closer of the two planes, the one painted black. They had the cover off the engine and were peering at whatever was inside. The other plane was a dull green and had targets painted on it. Outside the hangar, sitting in a wooden chair, was a slim man, probably in his mid-twenties, with short black hair, a neat moustache, and a pipe clamped between his teeth. He looked up as I approached but didn't pay me much attention.

His uniform looked different from the others, so I

figured he was in charge.

"Corporal Wyman reporting, sir," I said, standing in front of him.

He took the pipe from his mouth and looked up at me. "Reporting for what?"

"Duty, sir. Major Billings sent me."

"Well, that's just grand," he said, rising and shaking my hand. "We've been under-manned for weeks. It's about time HQ got their act together. What do you know of airplanes?"

"Um, nothing. Sir."

He dropped my hand and frowned briefly. Then he smiled. "Well, you're another pair of hands, and that's what counts. I'll be your commanding officer, Lieutenant Broadmoor Huntington. That's the Kensington Huntingtons, not the Berkshire Huntingtons." The way he pronounced it, however, was LEFF-tenant and BARK-sheer. "But call me Brody, everyone does. I'm sure you've twigged by now that this is a small, informal base, so as long as you're not insubordinate, no one is going to censure you. Now let's go meet the boys."

He guided me into the hangar and the two men stepped off the bench they were standing on to look into the engine.

"Men, this is Corporal ... what was it?"

"Wyman."

"Corporal Wyman. He has been assigned to assist you."

One of the men, the older of the two, with slicked back blonde hair, a fuzzy upper lip, and a cigarette hanging from his mouth, stepped forward. He took the cigarette in his left hand and held out his right.

"Flight Sergeant William Moore," he said as we

shook hands.

The second man introduced himself as Air Mechanic First Class Conrad Whittard. He was red-haired and ruddy-faced, and not much older than me.

"I'll leave you to get acquainted," Body said, "while I suit up for the initiation flight. Is Mrs. Beeton ready?"

Sergeant Moor grinned and looked at me. "Tuned up, gassed up, and ready to roll, sir."

"Excellent. Show young Wyman the ropes. I'll be back in a tick. Cheerio."

With that he sauntered away, to a smaller shed a short distance from the hangar. I watched him go.

"That's the Lieutenant's ready room," Moore said, when he saw where I was looking. "He's going to take Mrs. Beeton up."

"Mrs. Beeton?"

He pointed at the green plane.

"He's going to fly that?" I said, unable to hide my astonishment.

Both Moore and Whittard chuckled.

"Yes, indeed he is," Moore said. "Now, what sort of engines have you worked on?"

"None."

They both shook their heads and folded their arms.

"But I'm eager to learn, and I catch on fast."

Moore shook his head again. "Okay, corporal. This is how it's going to be. You outrank young Whittard there, but he can strip an engine after breakfast and have it back together, purring like a kitten, by dinnertime. Until you can do that, you take orders from him, as well as me, and Brody. Understood?"

I nodded. "Yes, sir."

"Your instruction will start as soon as your initiation is over."

I didn't like the sound of that. "My ...?"

Then I heard someone come up behind me. I turned and saw Brody, wearing a full-length, leather coat with a fur collar. On his head was a leather helmet and goggles. He had a white scarf around his neck and a pair of long, leather gloves in one hand. Draped over his arm was another leather coat with a pair of goggles balanced on top.

"Time to suit up, Wyman," he said tossing the coat at me.

"What's this for?" I asked, bending to pick up the goggles.

"Your flight suit. You want to go flying with me, don't you?"

From the smirks on all three of their faces, I realized this wasn't an offer I was meant to refuse.

Chapter 14

Charlie

In the few moments of solitude between Major Billings and Mitch leaving and Captain Jeffreys returning, I looked at the bullet, and a million thoughts went through my mind.

As adventures went, this one really wasn't going that badly. Mitch was right; we might have been conscripted into the army again, but no one was trying to kill us, and we did have flush toilets and a bed. All we needed to do was bide our time and wait for an opportunity to get back home. But that's where the danger was.

We were in a world of shit back home—grounded-for-the-summer type shit. Granddad's gift had set Mom off, but losing her jewellery box would push her over the edge. And add to that the missing bullet and there would be no explaining our way out of maximum confinement. Mom and Dad couldn't help but assume we'd hid them, and I didn't want to be mowing the lawn, trimming shrubs, and doing bullshit home-improvement projects for something we hadn't done. But if I could bring the bullet back and confess to breaking her box to get at it, at least we'd be punished for something we'd actually done. I felt I could live with that. Which was why, when Captain Jeffreys stepped into the office, I said, "Now that we have completed our mission, I will need to retake possession of the bullet."

Jeffreys stopped and looked at me. "Sergeant?"

"You have removed the incendiary material," I continued, trying to look calm, "and my orders are to not allow the bullet out of my sight. I assume you have no further need of it."

Captain Jeffreys nodded. "That is correct. The slug is now empty, the casing was always empty, so we have no further need of it."

To my relief, he picked up the bullet and handed it to me.

"And seeing as you are now a member of our little group," he said, as I stuffed the bullet into my pocket, "you should have a tour of the facility."

He guided me out of the office and stopped at his workbench. Behind it and under it were wooden shelves laden with containers of different coloured powders.

"This is where the magic happens," he said, smiling. "I am the principal chemist." He looked to the middle of the long room, where Major Billings was talking to one of the other two men. "Our friend, Major Billings, the team leader, is also a chemist, though the main responsibility for developing an adequate incendiary mixture is largely down to me."

"And that has been difficult?" I asked.

Jeffreys nodded, his smile gone. "Very much so. You have no idea how much I, and Major Billings, are relieved by your arrival." As he spoke, he took the three test tubes from the rack and poured the powders into a glass beaker. "A breakthrough before the next Zeppelin raid is paramount. Naturally, I would have preferred to have developed the formula myself, but I am a pragmatist, and any help I get helps the government and, ultimately …" He added the pile of powder from the metal plate to the beaker, then stirred it with a glass rod. "… the world."

After listening to his speech, I had only one question: "Zeppelins?"

He stopped peering into the beaker and looked at me, frowning. "Do you not know of them?"

"I'm afraid we don't hear much about them in the States."

"Canada, Sergeant. Canada."

"Sorry," I said. "But the Zeppelins, what are they? And what does all this," I swept my arm to indicate the rest of the lab, "have to do with them?"

"A good question, sergeant. Keep your eyes and ears open and all will be revealed."

He led me to the shelves and pointed at the containers, some wood, some metal, others just burlap bags. "These are the chemicals I work with. That one makes the incendiary mixture glow red, that one yellow, that one blue, and if I mix those two, green. For the incendiary mixture is not simply to set something on fire, it also conveys information, and assists in aiming. My remit is to make the mixture glow brighter, last longer, and burn hotter. That is the purpose of this base. Once we perfect a formula, and test it using a few, local airbases, the munitions factories can produce as many Buckingham bullets as you please, but unless we can supply them with an improved incendiary mixture, no one is going to take down a Zeppelin."

"Why not?"

Jeffreys picked up the beaker, put his free hand on my back, and guided me toward the rest of the lab.

"All in good time, sergeant."

We walked past other shelves, containing more chemicals, dozens of boxes of bullet components— dull, lead slugs and bright, brass casings—tools, and machine parts, to where a skinny man was bent over a strange-looking device. It was the man Billings had been talking to, though now the major was heading toward the far end of the lab. The man stood straight as we approached. He was just a shade taller than me, but thinner, with brown hair and a pale complexion.

"Captain Farber," Jeffreys said, "this is Sergeant Wyman, a young Canadian who has just joined our ranks. He will be replacing Captain Newell's assistant."

Farber's eyes narrowed as he shook my hand. "I trust you'll be staying longer."

Jeffreys coughed into his fist. "Farber, why don't you show young Wyman what it is you do?"

Farber's work area was as cluttered as Jeffrey's. In addition to his machine, which looked like some sort of stamping device, with a long, upright handle that he had been pressing down, there were boxes of slugs with holes bored into the blunt ends, a large glass beaker filled with powder and, on the far end, racks containing dozens of slugs with their holes packed full.

Farber grunted. "My job is simple. All it requires is a steady hand and a security clearance." He glared at Jeffreys as he said it, perhaps daring him to prove whether I had clearance or not. Jeffreys ignored him. "This scoop," Farber continued, picking up a small, metal measuring spoon, "delivers the proper amount of mixture into the packer." He scooped powder from the bowl, flipped open a tab on his machine and emptied what was in the spoon into what I assumed was some sort of hopper. Then he put a bullet into a slot in the base of the device and eased the lever down. As the hopper and the bullet met, Farber pressed harder, then he released the handle and removed the bullet, now filled with the compressed mixture.

"There you are," he said, holding the slug between his index and thumb. "A fully functioning Buckingham bullet."

"Not quite," Jeffreys said, setting his medium sized beaker on the bench and pushing the larger one aside. "This is a new mixture that we need to test. Can you make us a dozen or so?"

Farber nodded and set to work. He was surprisingly fast and had a dozen in one of the racks in minutes.

"Good man," Jeffreys said, picking up one of the bullets and inspecting it. "There's still one step to go." He pointed to the racks that had been filled before we got there. "You can dispose of those. And don't bother making any more of these until we test them."

Farber nodded. "I'll dispose of the old mixture, as well, then. So, it doesn't become confused with the new one."

"Excellent," Jeffreys said. "Carry on. Sergeant, follow me. And bring those bullets."

I nodded to Captain Farber, picked up the rack and went after Jeffreys. The bullets rattled in their wire holders, and I held my breath, hoping I wouldn't spill them all over the floor. The other man, who Major Billings was now talking to, was way down at the extreme end of the lab, so it was a long, tense walk.

"Captain Newell," Jeffreys said to the man standing at the workbench next to Major Billings, "meet your new assistant, Sergeant Wyman, fresh from the Canadian army."

Thankfully, Jeffreys took the bullet rack from me before Captain Newell grabbed my hand and began enthusiastically shaking it. "Always happy to welcome one of our cousins from across the pond." He was about my height, with a round face, short blonde hair, and a work area that was noticeably neater than Farber's or Jeffreys'. There were the standard wooden shelves nearby, but the pillow-sized burlap bags they contained were laid out end to end, spaced apart in tidy rows, and all that was on his workbench, aside from his machine, was a deep, oblong bowl with thick, metal sides, and a wooden box filled with empty shell casings.

"These are bullets with the new mixture," Jeffreys said, placing the rack on the counter.

"If you'll finish them off," Billings said, "we can perform some preliminary tests."

Newell nodded. "Won't be a tick. This way, Wyman, watch and learn."

The others stepped back as Newell dipped into the metal bowl and came up with a pinch of what looked like short pieces of uncooked spaghetti. He transferred this to a small saucer on the end of a tiny see-saw with a weight on the opposite end. As he added broken bits of spaghetti, the weight rose. When the see-saw was level, he took the narrow saucer, which had a sort of spout on one end, and tipped the pieces into a shell casing.

"That's the proper charge," he said, turning his head my way. "Once you get the hang of it, you won't need the scale, but make sure you use it until you know what you are doing."

I nodded, struggling to appear calm. "Yes, sir."

"Now, all we need to do is place the casing in this," he said, opening a clamp and setting the casing into it. "And then attach one of the bullets." He carefully lifted one of the slugs from the rack, put it in another clamp on his device and, like Captain Farber, pulled a lever down. Slowly. As the two parts came together, he inspected the joint, then pushed down hard until I heard a faint click.

Newell nodded and looked at me again. "That sound means the slug has been firmly clamped to the casing.

I nodded again.

"Now you," he said, stepping aside.

I felt my face go white. "Me?"

Newell laughed. "Don't worry son. I'll walk you through it."

With Newell guiding me, I fished out some of the spaghetti and put it on the scale until it levelled out. Then, my hand trembling, I tried to tip the pieces into a casing, spilling half of it on the counter.

I yelped and jumped back.

"Easy, son," Newell said. "There's no danger. Just pick up the pieces and put them in the casing."

Concentrating on my task helped calm me. I locked the casing, and the bullet, into the device without a problem.

"Now pull the lever down slowly," Newell said, "just until they meet. Then have a look to make sure they are exactly lined up."

I pulled, looked, asked Newell to look, then began applying more pressure.

"Did your last assistant really blow himself up?" I asked, after the device issued a satisfying click.

"Ah, poor Sergeant Rutherford," Newell said, shaking his head. "He was keen, but careless. He over-filled a casing, didn't check the seal properly, and accidentally set off the primer while the bullet was still in the device."

"Scared us all half to death," Jeffreys said.

"Thought the whole place might go up," Billings added. "The men managed to contain the blaze, or the explosion would have been seen from Redhill."

For the first time, I noticed that the clamps, and a number of other parts on Newell's device, were shiny and new, while the rest was dulled with age.

"Did he … is he … dead?"

"No," Newell said, unlatching the completed bullet. "They say he'll keep one of his eyes, and he only lost three of his fingers—two from his left hand, one from his right."

I took a breath. "He was lucky, then."

Newell nodded. "Yes …"

"But?"

"Well, he won't be winning any beauty contests."

I looked again at the burned patch on the workbench and the half-new, half-old device.

"You've nothing to worry about," Newell said, holding the bullet out to me. "Look here, your first bullet. And it's top-notch. Now let's get cracking. We need to finish the rest if we're going to do some proper testing."

"Carry on, then," Billings said. "We'll get the range set up, and the target inflated. You fill a few of those pans with the proper ammunition and meet us on the range."

He pointed to a rack on the other side of the room. On it were stacks of black metal disks, each about two inches thick and a foot in diameter. And next to the rack, lying on a large, sturdy table, were two huge machine guns.

◆

After crimping the rest of the bullets, I was less nervous, and then Newell showed me how to load the pans, which was what he called the metal disks, because that's what they looked like. On one side, the black metal had indents fanning out from a solid centre, and on the other side, they were open, so if you put a handle on it, you could imagine using it to cook pancakes.

The slots and the solid centre were used to hold the bullets, and loading them into the pans was a little tricky. You had to rotate the centre part using a special metal rod and slip the bullets, with their noses pointed toward the centre, into the indents. The pan held forty-seven shells, but we only loaded a few bullets into a couple of them, each with a different sort of ammunition.

Then Newell led me out to the shooting range, me balancing a stack of half a dozen pans, which was really heavy, and Newell with the much heavier machine gun, which he called a Lewis gun, slung over his shoulder.

We walked all the way to the far side of the base, into the corner where there were a few huts and a bench outside one of them. We were next to the fence, away from all the buildings, with a clear view to the other side of the base, where a huge balloon—

tethered by several ropes attached to cement blocks—floated about twenty feet in the air. Waiting for us at the bench were Major Billings, Captain Jeffreys and Captain Farber.

"Jeffreys tells me you don't know what a Zeppelin is," Billings said as we drew near.

I looked at the balloon and made a guess. "It's an airship, like a blimp," I said, setting the pans on the bench.

Billings nodded. "A big airship. One we have no defence against."

Our conversation was put on hold as an engine that had been idling in the background suddenly revved up. I looked and saw an airplane coming our way, bouncing and roaring, before lifting from the ground and soaring over our heads.

We all looked up. It was a two-seater. In the rear was a man I didn't recognize, and in the front seat—recognizable even wearing a helmet and goggles—was Mitch.

"Taking the new lad up for a ride," Newell said.

"He'd best be back before he needs to take the new bullets to Suttons Farm," Jeffreys said.

I watched the plane climb, do a loop, and for the first time felt glad I had been given the dangerous job.

Billings looked at me.

"Are they doing a lot of damage?" I asked, to get the conversation rolling again.

Billings shook his head. "Overall, they do very little. The German bombers do more physical damage, but the psychological damage caused by the Zeppelins is much worse."

"How so?"

As Jeffreys and Newell checked the pans and set

the Lewis gun up with an inverted V-shaped support under its barrel, Billings explained:

"People know what an airplane is, and we can shoot them down. But a Zeppelin is five hundred feet long, sixty feet wide, and can fly from forty to sixty miles an hour, at twelve thousand feet. We've got nothing on the ground that can shoot that high, and our planes can barely attain that altitude. At night the Zeppelins are practically invisible, and almost silent, so finding one is nearly impossible. And if one of our planes manages to catch up with one and get close enough for a shot, well, it doesn't do much good. They are, as far as the people are concerned, invincible. And that is causing panic."

"The people look upon them as Satan himself," Farber said. "They are so frightened they are pressuring the Government to drop out of the war. And if another fleet of Zeppelins comes and goes with their usual impunity, that's just what is going to happen."

Billings grimaced. "Perhaps. But it is up to us to make sure it doesn't come to that."

"But they're just balloons," I said. "I know it's hard to find them, but once you do, can't you just pop them with a few bullets?"

"These aren't toy balloons, son," Billings said. "They don't 'pop.' Inside each Zeppelin, there are nineteen individual gas bags—much bigger than that one floating over there—and a bullet merely makes a pinprick in it that the Germans can fix without a problem. What we need is a way to set them on fire."

I looked at the balloon, which as Billings noted, was really a big canvas bag filled with gas, and imagined holding a Bic lighter up to it. "How can you do that if they're flying so high and so fast?"

"What keeps a Zeppelin in the air is a million cubic feet of hydrogen gas," Billings said. "And hydrogen is flammable. A spark could set off a chain reaction that would blow the Zeppelin sky high." He smiled, "Or, in this case, sky higher."

"And this is what we've been working on," Jeffreys said, setting a pan on top of the Lewis gun, then turning it until it clicked. "There are, however, challenges." Newell got behind the Lewis gun and aimed it, while Jeffreys continued. "The Buckingham bullets contain a phosphorus compound that burns, producing a line of smoke, or a trace. But there's a problem." He looked up at the balloon. "This is about as close as you would want to get to a Zeppelin. Now watch."

Newell pulled the trigger. The gun bucked and a line of smoke left the barrel, heading for the balloon, then fizzled out.

"See there?" Jeffreys said, as Newell removed the pan from the Lewis gun and attached a different one. "The phosphorus doesn't burn long enough to reach the hydrogen. But the new formula I devised may fix that."

I nodded, pleased at how naturally he stuck to the story.

"That first bullet went out before it hit the bag. This one should reach it while still burning. Now watch."

He nodded to Newell who took aim. I looked at the balloon floating above the field and put my hands over my ears. The gun roared. A streak of smoke shot toward the balloon, went into it and out the other side. And the balloon continued to float.

I lowered my hands.

"What just happened? Why didn't it explode?"

Jeffreys smiled. "Chemistry."

Chapter 15

Mitch

Whittard spun the propeller and Brody, in the seat behind me, worked the controls until the engine hummed.

"Ready?" Brody asked.

He grinned at me as I turned and gave him a nod and a thumbs-up, grateful that I hadn't eaten anything since breakfast, as I assumed whatever was left in my stomach was about to come up.

Brody nodded in return, revved the engine to a deafening roar, and the plane began to move. Fast, then faster. It bounced and jolted and threw me against my harness and then, suddenly, the wheels left the ground and it felt like we were floating on a cushion of air, which I suppose we were.

The ground fell away. I looked down as we passed the perimeter fence and saw, on one side, Charlie, Billings, Jeffreys and two other men standing around a machine gun, and on the other side, a canvas balloon hovering at our height, some distance away. Then I looked forward, as Brody drove the plane upwards toward the clouds. We climbed for a few moments, then I saw the sun, the sky, the base, the trees. I felt my harness tighten, then slacken, and realized we had just done a loop. It was thrilling, and the lump of ice in my stomach melted away, leaving a tingle of excitement.

The plane, although flimsy looking, felt solid, almost invincible, in the air. Brody had already shown me some of what it could do. I looked forward to more.

We climbed higher and I tried to take everything in, wishing the wings didn't block part of the view. Up in the sky there was only the drone of the engine, and us. The ground looked like a patchwork quilt, and I could see the countryside for miles around. I looked up at the sky and the clouds as they zipped by. It was freezing, but I didn't care. Then the horizon flipped, and I was looking straight up at the ground, and I realized Brody was flying upside-down. I was startled for a moment, but the harness held me securely so there was nothing to worry about.

I turned as far as I could, until I could see Brody, grinning at me from beneath his goggles. I shouted that I didn't know airplanes could fly upside down. His smile faltered and he pointed the plane straight up and we looped over in a big circle. Then he pointed the airplane down, and the ground screamed toward us until he pulled the nose of the plane up, which pushed me down into my seat. We were going really fast now, and Brody spun the plane so it rolled over and over. I saw sky, land, sky, land, sky, land, and it was so dizzying I laughed out loud.

It was marvellous; it was miraculous. To think that something made of wood and material and a noisy engine could fly so high, so fast, and turn so quickly. It was miles better than riding in a car.

Brody made the plane climb higher, until the ground disappeared in the haze of clouds. We sailed along in the freezing fog, then came out into blazing sunshine. Below, the patchwork had merged into the green of the countryside, and the darker areas that signified towns. I tried to get my bearings, and figured the base was far behind us, and the huge stain spreading over the land in front of us was London. Then I saw the silver snake of a river that had to be the Thames.

"London!" I said, pointing.

I looked back at Brody. He was frowning.

"What?" I shouted. "Did I get that wrong?"

Brody shook his head, did a couple of barrel-rolls, then turned the plane one hundred and eighty degrees, going into a speedy dive as he did. We flew closer to the ground so I could see the houses and villages. I knew we were heading south, so when I saw a large town, I was sure it was Redhill. Then, to the other side, I saw a flash of light, as if something had flared up and fizzled out.

"That's Redhill," I shouted. Then I pointed to where I had seen the flash. "And our base is over there."

I turned to look at Brody again, who had a quizzical expression on his face. Then he turned the plane, and we headed home. He eased it down slowly. Soon, the base came into view. As we neared, I saw Charlie and the others, but the balloon was gone.

We flashed over the fence, dropped to the earth, and the bone-shaking rattle began again. It smoothed out soon enough, however, and Brody idled the plane up to the hangar, where Whittard and Moore were waiting. As the engine died, I took off my goggles and helmet and climbed out of my seat.

Whittard ran over to assist Brody while Moore came to help me, his grin fading as I climbed out of the plane with a smile on my face. As soon as I was on the ground, I saw Charlie and Billings coming our way. I was about to call out to Charlie when Brody stepped in front of me.

"How did you know that was London?" he asked.

I shrugged. "It was obvious, wasn't it? Big city. With a river."

"And Redhill? And the base?"

I looked at him, trying to figure out if he was angry or not. "Well, we were heading in that direction. And given our speed, it was most likely Redhill. And the base is near Redhill. When I saw the flash, I knew that was it."

Brody shook his head. "You were supposed to be too preoccupied with vomiting and soiling yourself to think about airspeed and direction."

"Sorry," I said.

For the first time, Brody smiled. "Don't be," he said, then turned to face Billings.

Chapter 16

Charlie

"What do you mean?"

Newell attached a different pan to the Lewis gun while Jeffreys continued watching the balloon. There were now two small holes in it, but it didn't seem to be affecting it.

"What do you need to start a fire?" he asked.

I shrugged. "Something to burn. And something to set it alight."

Jeffreys nodded. "Yes, but what else?"

I shook my head.

"Come now," Jeffreys said. "Remember your science lessons. What makes a fire burn. Or, more to the point, what would make it not burn?"

"I suppose, not having any air. Or oxygen."

"That's right. You could light a fire inside one of those gas bags and nothing would happen at all because there is no oxygen mixed with the hydrogen to allow it to burn."

"And that's where our friends Brock and Pomeroy come in," Newell said, looking down the sight of the Lewis gun. "They invented exploding bullets, which make larger holes in the bags, allowing the air to mix with the hydrogen."

Without warning, he pulled the trigger and the Lewis gun bucked and rattled, spitting out line after line of smoke. It was over in a second, and when I looked at the balloon there was a visible hole about one third of the way up from the bottom.

I turned to Jeffreys. "What just happened?"

"The Brock bullets explode on impact. Just a little. Enough to make a small hole, but if you concentrate your fire into one place, it will produce an opening large enough to exploit."

"The instinct of the pilots, though," Billings said, "is to strafe the Zeppelin, which does little good."

Jeffreys nodded. "Indeed. We need to impress upon them the importance of concentrating their Brock rounds. Then fire the Buckingham bullets into the same place."

"Not an easy feat," Billings said.

"An impossible one," Farber added.

"But theoretically doable," Newell said, as he again switched pans on the Lewis gun. "Now this pan magazine holds the first bullet you made. I think it would be appropriate if you fired the killing shot."

He grinned at me and stepped away from the gun.

"Me? But I—"

"Don't worry, sergeant. It's just like any other weapon you used in basic training."

I stepped up to the gun, trying hard to look like I knew what I was doing. Getting into the position I had seen Newell adopt, I pointed the barrel at the balloon and pressed the trigger. The gun shuttered and the stock slammed into my shoulder and the barrel jumped into the air and my bullet missed.

"Sorry," I said, watching the trace from my bullet—well wide of the target—drift away.

Newell placed his hand on my shoulder. "Don't worry, lad. It's just a shame you missed with your

111

inaugural bullet." He pulled the pan off the gun and replaced it with one of the others. "This has more of the new rounds in it, but why don't you let me have a go this time?"

Gratefully, I stood aside.

Newell aimed. A shot rang out. Smoke zipped toward the hole the Brock bullets had made. And the balloon exploded, lighting the sky with a ball of yellow flame. A second later a wave of hot air swept over me.

Newell stood and shook Jeffreys's hand. "Well done. I think you've cracked it."

Jeffreys nodded. "There's more work to be done, but these will do for now."

"And we need to deliver them today in case the pilots are called out for a night raid," Billings said.

Farber headed for the lab. "I will get started on that immediately," he said.

Billings nodded. "Good man. You two, find some soldiers to help clean up the debris, and get this equipment back to the lab."

"Yes sir."

Farber hurried off, while Newell and Jeffreys went in search of idle soldiers.

"Sergeant Wyman," Billings said, "you and I will visit the hangar to see when we might expect Lieutenant Huntington to return."

"I think that might be them now," I said, looking over my shoulder.

In the distance, it was just possible to hear the faint burr of an engine, then I saw a dot coming through the sky, getting closer.

"That does appear to be him," Billings said. "With me, sergeant. I need a word with Lieutenant

112

Huntington, and your brother may need your assistance."

"Why so?" I asked as we started across the field.

"The lieutenant enjoys taking his new recruits up for a spin. Most of them come back a little wobbly."

The plane flew low over the fence, bounced on the grass, then taxied to the hangar, and we followed. When Mitch got out, he didn't look wobbly. In fact, it looked like he was smiling. Lieutenant Huntington stepped in front of him as we approached, and they appeared to be talking, which made me wonder if something was wrong, but when he stepped aside and turned to Billings, it was clear that Mitch was fine.

Then the lieutenant said, "Major Billings, meet your new pilot."

Chapter 17

Mitch

"What?" both Major Billings and I said at once.

Brody put a hand on my shoulder. "This lad is the most natural airman I have ever met. He has a gift. It would be a crime not to use it."

Billings shook his head. "That's impossible."

Surprisingly, a dart of disappointment speared my chest. I should have been relieved. The flight had been magnificent, but I wasn't a pilot. I could never be a pilot. Even so, the thought took hold in my mind and refused to be rooted out.

Then Brody took a step toward Billings. "I think you'll find it's not only possible, but highly probable."

Was it? To be in an airplane was magic. To fly one, what must that be like? Could it happen? Should it happen?

"But he's … Canadian."

"And a natural," Brody said. "This is what he was born to do. And we need all the airmen we can get. Canadian or not."

Billings' face was red now. Charlie just stood with his mouth open.

"He can't be a pilot," Billings said. "He's a corporal. You need to be an officer to be a pilot."

Brody smiled and shook his head. "All right then, I'm promoting him to Second Lieutenant."

"You can't do that."

"I just did."

"I will not—"

"I think you will," Brody said. Then his voice softened. "We're all on the same team. There's no need to be territorial. Second Lieutenant Wyman has been assigned to me, so you obviously don't need him. If I train him to be a pilot, you've lost nothing, the service gets one more—if I judge him correctly—damn fine pilot, and everyone wins."

Billings took a deep breath. "All this needs to be cleared—"

"Leave that to me," Brody said. "Now then, Second Lieutenant Wyman, we'll need to get you a proper uniform."

That seemed to signal a dismissal for Billings. His face turned a little red, then he barked. "See that your airplane is fit and ready. You have a delivery to make before the sun sets."

Brody saluted. "Yes, sir."

That seemed to satisfy Billings. He returned the salute and left, calling, "With me, sergeant," as he went.

Before he left to catch up with Billings, Charlie turned to me, a smirk on his face. "Congratulations, Second Lieutenant Wyman."

I felt my face glow, and I couldn't help grinning. Charlie would think it was because I now outranked him, but I couldn't have cared less about that. I had found my place. That's what I was smiling about.

Chapter 18
Sunday, 27 August 1916

Charlie

The next morning, after breakfast, I reported to Captain Newell, and found him cleaning his crimping device in an empty laboratory.

The two of us, along with Farber, had worked the previous afternoon to make as many bullets as we could from the remaining mixture. We'd managed to fill seven pans, which I delivered to Lieutenant Huntington who, with Whittard in the observer's seat cradling the pans in a burlap sack, flew away with them.

I hadn't seen Mitch.

In the early evening, we ate in the mess hall, a building half as large as the lab, on the other side of the base. I was at the Non-Commissioned Officers' table with the rest of the NCOs: Sergeants Dobson and Orr, Corporals Blake and Rawlings, Flight Sergeant Moore, and Air Mechanic First Class Whittard. Mitch sat at the officers' table, even though he was still in his corporal uniform. It must have been awkward, but at least he had Lieutenant Huntington to back him up. Though, come to think of it, the captains didn't seem to have anything against him; it was just Major Billings, and I thought that might have more to do with Annie than our unconventional arrival. After all, Billings seemed okay with me.

The enlisted men sat at the largest table. There were about seventy-five soldiers in all, and it made me wonder why Billings complained about being understaffed, but then what do I know about running a secret military base?

After the meal, I was shown to my quarters, a room so tiny Dobson apologized, but noted that, if things had turned out differently, I'd be sharing it with Mitch. Mitch, naturally, was assigned officers' quarters. I had no idea what his room looked like, but I was sure it was better than mine. No use complaining about it, however. That was one thing I had learned about the army. Another was to always look busy, which was why I had reported to Newell before someone ordered me to do something else.

"No work for you today," he said, as I approached. "We've made all the bullets we can with the new formula, and there's no sense in making any with the old formula."

"Then what should I do?"

Newell put down the oily rag he was using. "You can help me tidy up. A shipment came in for me this morning." He pointed to a pallet stacked with what looked like sandbags but which I knew were sacks of exploding stuff (or 'propellant' as Newell called it). "And there's a pile of used pan magazines someone dumped back there. If you could stack them neatly, I'd appreciate it."

It was something to do, and it beat digging a latrine pit, which is what I usually ended up doing when I was conscripted into one army or another. Stacking the pans was easy. The sacks were another story. They were small, but unwieldy, and they had been dumped in a pile, so removing them was like playing Jenga. I carried them one at a time to the shelving unit and laid them carefully end to end, terrified I might drop one. Until I did.

On my fifth trip, the sack slipped from my hands and landed on the cement floor. I screamed and jumped back, causing Newell to turn so fast he knocked his chair over. Then he laughed.

"Easy, son. There's no danger."

"But," I said, still shaking, "it's explosive."

Newell righted his chair and came over to me. "Only when it's enclosed." He bent and picked up the bag, passing it from hand to hand as if it didn't weigh anything. "In this state, it would only burn. Bad enough, and not something you would want to happen but, unlike gunpowder, you can hit this with a hammer, drop it from a great height, or run it over with a truck, and it won't explode."

"What is it?"

"Cordite," he said. "A remarkable substance. It will burn when wet, and doesn't smoke as much as gunpowder."

"Seriously?" I asked, as he continued to pass the bag from hand to hand.

"Absolutely." He gave the bag to me, and I struggled to hold it nonchalantly. "Leave the rest of them for me. Let's you and I make a few more bullets."

"But I thought—"

"And you were right," he said, walking away. "But this is something different."

I laid the bag of cordite out, then joined Newell, who was at Captain Farber's workstation.

"Major Billings wants to know the range of the

new bullets," he said, taking up the empty beaker. "After filling all the pans yesterday, there were six bullets left over. If we can get a few more out of this, that should be enough to do our range testing."

"But it's empty," I said.

Newell held the beaker at an angle and tapped the base on the workbench. "Oh, there's always a drop or two left in the bottle. Here, look."

A small amount of powder had jarred loose from the sides. Just a bit.

"That's enough for a few," he said, and set to work with the scoop.

In a short time, he had filled three bullets.

"Now, why don't you try," he said, as he placed the last one in the rack.

"Because I'm liable to blow the lab up?" I guessed.

Newell chuckled as he turned to a nearby shelf and pulled a half-empty bag from it.

"This is an inert substance," he said, pouring yellow powder into the beaker. "There's no danger."

After some basic instruction, he let me try on my own.

"The key is to avoid anything that might precipitate a rapid incendiary event."

"Meaning, blowing up the lab?"

"Exactly. Now, you're doing fine. Steady on."

I filled one bullet. It wasn't perfect, but Newell didn't criticize. The second one looked better. I had started on a third when Newell spoke.

"The word is that you and your brother are not what you seem to be."

I struggled to keep my hand, and my voice, steady.

"What word is that?"

"That you show up with the Major's niece, and

suddenly you're NCOs in the British army."

"There's nothing strange about that. We were transferred here."

"And a day later your bother is a Second Lieutenant."

I shrugged. "I guess Lieutenant Huntington took a liking to him."

Newell nodded. "And you say, LOO tenant, not LEFT tenant."

"We grew up near the American border. Their culture sorta seeped across."

"And you're a sergeant in the army, but you've never fired a weapon before."

I pressed down the lever. "So, what are you saying?"

"I'm saying nothing. I'm just telling you what the men think."

I turned to face him.

"And what do they think?"

"They think you might be criminals, using the army to shield you. Or agents from the War Office sent here to ascertain our progress. Or spies."

"And what do you think?"

Newell smiled. "I don't think anything. But I do know you've never held a rifle before. And that you should mind your pronunciations."

I turned back to the machine to get it ready to fill another bullet.

"That's enough for now, sergeant," Newell said. "You're dismissed. I will send for you when I need you."

I left the lab, my head buzzing. Was Newell threatening me, or simply advising me to blend in better? I decided I needed to talk to Mitch about it, so

I headed for the hangar. Lieutenant Huntington was nowhere to be seen, but Whittard and Moore were working on the black plane, and they told me Mitch was going into town with the Major's niece, and that I might be able to catch him at the front gate.

I hurried away and arrived just as an ancient automobile with a Taxi sign on it sputtered to a halt. Mitch was waiting inside, wearing a different uniform, one with lieutenant bars on it. Annie, as she got out of the cab, stopped and gaped.

"Mitch," I called, running up behind him as the guards opened the gate. "Where are you going?"

Before Mitch could take a step, Annie ran up to him and grabbed his hands. "Look at you. An officer. How—"

"Ma'am, you are not allowed inside the perimeter," one of the guards said. "Please step away."

Annie backed up, pulling Mitch with her. I followed.

"Sergeant," the guard called. "Show your pass."

"I'm not going anywhere," I said. "I just need to talk to my brother."

"Then step inside."

I took a step back. There was less than a yard between us, but Mitch and Annie were outside the base, and I was inside, and that seemed to satisfy the guards. That's the army for you.

"What are you doing?" I asked.

"Going into town," Mitch said. "Horsham. Why don't you come too."

Behind him, Annie's face fell.

"But Major Billings," I said. "How did you get a pass from him," I waved toward Annie, "for this?"

"Grandmother had a word with him," Annie said.

I looked at Annie. "Maggie?"

"She can be very persuasive."

"And you're an officer," I said to Mitch. "How on earth did that happened. Major Billings was dead against it, and the men—"

"I don't know," Mitch said. "Brody—"

"Who's Brody?" Annie asked.

Mitch turned to her. "My new CO. Broadmoor Huntington."

"Of the Kensington Huntingtons?"

Mitch shook his head. "The Bark Sheer Huntingtons."

Annie nodded. "Oh. That explains it."

And she said nothing further, as if that actually did explain it.

"So, are you coming?" Mitch asked.

I hesitated. I needed to talk to Mitch, and I really wouldn't have minded going with them, but the look on Annie's face told me she'd rather I didn't. Fortunately, after a few awkward moments, Newell saved the day.

"There you are, sergeant," he said, walking up to the gate. "I think it's time we tested that ammunition."

So, I said goodbye to Mitch, and a much-relieved Annie, and went with Captain Newell.

It took a while to get everything set up. We went back to the range, but there was no big bag of hydrogen, just a bundle of sticks, which I had to pound into the ground at fifty-foot intervals, while Newell got the Lewis gun and the bullets.

The bench was no longer there, either. He set the Lewis gun on the ground, with the supporting V under the barrel, and laid down behind it. Taking a single bullet, he loaded it into the pan, and attached the pan to the machine gun.

"This is one of the old bullets. So we can see where we were. Keep watch now."

He fired, and a streak of smoke shot past the markers.

"It stopped between seven hundred and fifty and eight hundred feet," I said.

Newell nodded. "Yes, around two-hundred and fifty yards. That had been our best effort. The new bullets traced passed the target, which was three-hundred and fifty yards away, and went on for a bit longer." He loaded another round into the pan. "This is one of the new ones. Keep an eye on the trace."

He fired. The smoke fizzled out before the fifth marker.

"That's barely five hundred feet," I said.

Newell frowned. "It could have been a dud. I'll try another."

He loaded another bullet and fired, with the same results.

"That's odd," he said, staring down the range. "I must have mixed up the old and new bullets."

He took one of the three he had made that morning and locked it in.

"Keep a sharp eye, sergeant," he called. "We've only three chances."

He fired. The trace extended to just over two hundred feet.

Newell frowned and stood up. "This is serious," he said. "Very serious, indeed."

He paced behind the Lewis gun, his hands in his pockets, looking at the ground.

"You stay here," he said after a while. "Guard the

machine gun, and the bullets. I'm going to get Major Billings."

He handed me the bullets—four left over from the previous night in one hand, and two he'd just made in the other—and set off at a fast walk.

He returned a few minutes later with Billings and Jeffreys. Billings wasted no words.

"Show us, sergeant," he said before they had even reached me.

I gulped. "Old or new?" I asked.

"The ones made this morning," he said. "It's the only way we can be certain it was from the new mixture."

I sighed and pulled one of the morning's bullets from my pocket.

"Here," Newell said. "I'll handle that. You watch the markers."

Relieved, I handed him the bullet and stood to the side, away from the group. The trace from the shot fizzled at the two-hundred-foot marker.

They ended up shooting all the rounds, and all the results were the same.

Newell stood, his hands on his hips, staring down the range, looking perplexed. Billings looked disgusted; Jeffreys looked dumbfounded.

"What," Billings said, glaring at Jeffreys, "is going on?"

Jeffreys shook his head. "I don't know. The mixture, it must have degraded over time. That is not something I would have considered possible."

"Unless my eyes deceive me," Billings said, "then it jolly well is possible."

"So, what do we do?" Newell asked.

"Nothing," Billings said. "We tell no one and do

nothing."

"But we've sent Buckingham ammunition to the pilots," Jeffreys said. "Ammunition that—"

"Is no better or worse than what they were already using. Letting this out will only encourage the men to distrust us. I've already told command that we had cracked it, and I'm not going to tell them I was mistaken. The only way anyone will know if anything is wrong with those bullets is if there is a Zeppelin raid. We just have to pray that none comes before you can make a proper mixture. And thoroughly test it."

"And when will that be?" Jeffreys said, his voice rising. "I need those chemicals."

Billings sighed. "I have ordered them, and I will tell them of the urgency, but you know as well as I do that badgering the quartermasters can sometimes be counterproductive."

Jeffreys ran a hand over his whitening face. "Henry, you know how critical—"

"Better than you. But for now, there is nothing to be done. In a few days, God willing, the boys will have the improved Buckingham bullets, and none of this will matter. Until such time, no one—and that means no one, not even Farber—knows that the bullets are duds. If this gets away from the four of us," here he looked straight at me, "I will know and I will hunt down the guilty party and make him rue the day of his birth. Clear?"

"Yes, Sir," I said, while Newell and Jeffreys nodded.

Billings walked away and Jeffreys joined him. It sounded like they were discussing production and how to further perfect the formula.

"There go the scientists," Newell muttered, "off to

save the world." Then he turned to me. "Gather the brass, sergeant."

"Shall I take down the range markers too?"

He shook his head. "No, they'll come in handy. Wait here while I go to the storage unit for a box of standard ammunition."

He set off, walking toward one of the nearby sheds. "What for?" I called after him.

"If you're going to insist on impersonating a soldier," he said, "you'll need to learn how to handle a Lewis gun."

Chapter 19

Mitch

We sat in the back seat, uncomfortably close to each other, as the cab bounced over the rutted road. I felt ridiculous in my new uniform. I had on a shirt and tie, and a khaki jacket with a wide leather belt around my waist and a thinner one that came over my right shoulder. The pants, a lighter shade of khaki, bunched out around my thighs, and the black leather boots came almost up to my knees. On my head, instead of the standard cap of an enlisted soldier, was a stiff hat with a brim and an insignia on the front. I felt like I was heading to a Halloween Party. Annie, on the other hand, wore a blue dress with ruffled sleeves, white gloves, and a purple sash around her waist. Her hair was curled and, although she wore a comically ostentatious hat, I couldn't think of her as anything but pretty.

Then it occurred to me that I had been staring at her for a long time, and it was getting awkward. I thought I ought to tell her how good she looked— and not mention the hat—but before I could, she said, "You look smashing in your uniform," and then I couldn't compliment her because she'd think I was only copying her. And then I realized I was still staring at her.

"Um, thanks," I said, because I couldn't think of

anything else to say.

"An officer," Annie said. "How?"

"I told you. Brody did it."

"But why?"

I shrugged. "He took me up in his airplane to scare me. As a sort of initiation. But it was amazing, and I wasn't scared a bit. So now he thinks I'm a natural pilot, and he wants to teach me to fly. When your uncle Henry told him he couldn't because I wasn't an officer, he made me a second lieutenant."

Her eyes widened. "A pilot! How exciting. And brave. Especially as you've never seen an airplane before."

That puzzled me. "What makes you think that?"

She glanced at the back of the driver's head and leaned close. "Well," she said, her voice low. "You're a knight, from an ancient kingdom. Airplanes don't exist where you come from."

I sighed. "I don't know why people keep saying that. I'm not a knight, I'm not from some ancient kingdom, and I've seen plenty of airplanes."

She leaned away; her brow furrowed. "Then where are you from."

And there it was, the question no one had ever asked.

Before thinking about the possible consequences, I told her. "The future." Then, to keep her from asking the next obvious question, I said, "The year two thousand and eighteen."

Her face went white, and her eyes widened. "A hundred years," she whispered. "One hundred and two years?"

I nodded. Now she would ask who won the war, and what happened after, and I thought of all the other wars, and nuclear weapons, and greenhouse gases, and struggled to think of what answers to give.

But, instead, she asked, "Do women get the vote?"

This threw me. I knew more about war than women's' rights.

"Yes," I said. I was certain of that, and also pretty sure her knowing about it wouldn't change the course of history.

She squealed with delight, making the driver glance in the rear-view mirror. I held my hands up in front of me to show him I wasn't the cause.

"When?" she asked, leaning close to my ear.

"I don't know. A long time ago. Or, a little while in the future for you."

"When?" she asked again.

"Well, the 19th, or 20th amendments. One of them gave women the vote. In the US. It was shortly after World War One, I think."

"One?"

Now I'd done it. "Look. Forget I said—"

Her face, no longer white, or pink with delight, turned a sickly grey that made me think she might faint. "What happens?" she asked, her voice rising. "What is coming for us?"

"I don't know," I said more sharply than I intended.

Two things happened in that moment. First, I realized I was right, and second, the driver yelled at us.

"If you two want to argue, I can let you out here so you can shout at each other in peace."

"It's all right," I said, struggling to keep my voice calm. I looked at Annie, who was slowly going from grey to white. "Every thing's fine."

The driver harrumphed but kept driving. Annie sat, staring forward, trembling as the thoughts tumbled around in my head.

"We'll talk on the train," I whispered. "Don't worry."

"Easy for you to say."

I thought of several answers, but none that wouldn't elicit a sharp response, and since I didn't feel like walking, I kept my mouth shut. Fortunately, we were dropped at the station a few minutes later. Once there, taking charge helped Annie calm down, and by the time she had bought tickets, hustled me onto a train and found an empty compartment, she was her old self, which made me wish I had been able to talk to her while she'd been terrified.

"What's going to happen," she demanded, as soon as she slammed the door.

I sat down opposite her. "I don't know."

Her face turned red. "How can you not know? You're from the future."

I nodded. "Yes, but whose future?" This confused her into silence for a moment, and I seized the opportunity. "I don't know why I'm here, but there must be a reason. Every summer, some power sends me, and my brother, back in time. To a significant event. And we meet Mr. Merwyn—"

"Who?"

"He's a Druid. He comes to us. Every time. But with different names. Once he was Malcolm, another time, Mendel, but he's always the same person. And then there's the Talisman, a black stone with great power that keeps the Land, England, safe."

I could see that I was confusing her. I paused, and she asked, "Why you?"

"Good question. We've never been called knights, but we have been called Guardians. Somehow, we're responsible for the Talisman. It's up to us to keep it safe, and to give it to whoever is supposed to have it. That's why we're here. England is in danger. The bullet we brought will help, but at some point, the Druid will appear, and he'll tell us where the Talisman is and what we need to do with it. That's our real mission."

"So, why then can't you tell me—"

"Because I think the future, your future, maybe even mine, depends on whether or not we succeed. One time, we arrived late. There was a battle, and we didn't get the Talisman in time, and we lost. I think we were supposed to win that battle, and I think losing it changed the course of history. So, I can't tell you who wins this war, because I don't know. It depends on what the Druid tells us when he finds us, and what happens with the Talisman."

She sat, her mouth open, her eyes fixed on mine. "You were in a battle?"

I nodded. As usual, details from our previous trips became vivid: the sights, the sounds, the smells, and the screams. "More than one," I said, my voice quaking. "It was horrific."

She sat on the seat next to me and put an arm over my shoulders. "I'm so sorry I called you a coward."

"Don't be," I said. "I'd love to be a coward. It's just that I keep getting shoved into these situations against my will. But somehow, I know what we're doing is important, so I don't have the luxury of being afraid."

She pulled me closer. "I'll help, if I can."

I wanted to tell her it wasn't her problem, and

131

there was nothing she could do, but then I thought of Kayla, and Ellen, and Pendragon, so I just said, "Thanks."

She gave me a quick hug, then moved away. "Now," she said, "tell me what women are treated like in your world."

The change in mood was so abrupt, I laughed. "Well, they can vote, for one. But they can also run for office. I think, if I remember right, in the nineteen eighties, you even had a woman Prime Minister."

"No," she said, slapping my arm. "You're having fun with me. That can't be."

"I swear, it's true. There are also women lawyers, doctors, astronauts—"

"What's an astronaut?"

"Ah, never mind. That's not important. The important thing is, women can do anything men can do."

For the rest of the trip, I drip-fed her facts about women in the twenty-first century. She was amazed by most of it, sceptical of some of it, and wanted to believe all of it. After we left the train, she took my arm as we walked into town, and steered the conversation toward current events and local gossip, which I thought was a clever move. It wouldn't be a good idea to have anyone overhear me describing something that hadn't been invented yet.

As we strolled through the Carfax and approached West Street, she became agitated, like she wanted to ask me something but was afraid to. Then she took a Votes For Women ribbon out of her pocketbook and pinned it to her dress. "I'd like you to talk at the meeting."

I stopped and turned to face her. "What meeting?"

"The meeting we're going to."

I looked at her ribbon. "You're taking me to a Suffragette meeting?"

Her eyes narrowed. "Where did you think we were going?"

"I don't know, but I wouldn't have guessed that. And I really don't want to talk to them."

She sighed, then looked straight into my eyes. "I know this is a surprise, and it's all rather sudden, but this is important to me, and to them, as important as the war. They believe, like I do, that we will triumph. We believe with hope in our hearts, and we encourage one another to keep that hope burning." She put her hands on my shoulders and pulled me closer. "But you, when you talk about it, you don't talk with hope, you talk with knowledge. There is strength in your words, because you know. Like when you told the crowd that America would enter the war. You weren't guessing, or hoping, or promising. You knew. That made your words carry weight."

"Not enough," I said, remembering the riot. "And, besides, I'm not a speaker, I can't do it."

She shook her head. "And you're not a pilot, but you're going to become one. You say you're not a hero, but you saved that woman and her baby. And you go off on these missions, without any idea what you're getting into. Surely you can say a few words to a group of women. It will make a difference. I know."

"I don't know. What if I slip up, and say something I shouldn't?"

She turned away and began pulling me down West Street. "You're smarter than that. Come on, we're already late."

We passed a shop with a display of old bicycles

133

and horse saddles outside, then stopped in front of a large building that looked like a drug store, which she called a Chemists, where she opened a door that led to a stairway. At the foot of the stairs, she turned to me.

"Whatever you do," she said, "do not use the word 'Suffragette.' We are Suffragists."

I stood close to her in the dim light, urging her to move on, wanting to get whatever it was she was getting me into, over with. "What's the difference?"

"It's a big difference," she said. "An important difference. I, and those like me, want equal rights for women. But we are determined to bring that about by peaceful means. The Suffragettes are the ones smashing windows, blowing up buildings and burning houses down."

"They're terrorists?" I asked, trying to recall if I had learned any of this in school.

"Yes," she said, her voice rising, and cracking a bit. "They've agreed to stop to help with the war effort, but people continue to confuse us with them, sometimes on purpose, so they can feel justified in attacking us. The Suffragettes have made it difficult to carry out our work. We believe change without violence is possible. But we won't get the chance to realize that because their violence has spilled onto us. We're tarred with the same brush, we're—"

Then her voice broke. It was too dim to see if she was crying, but she turned quickly away and ran a gloved hand over her face. "Just don't," she said, walking up the stairs.

"I won't," I said, following.

At the top of the stairs was a short hallway with two doors. Annie opened one of them and we stepped into a large room. We were at the back, so all I could see were hats and the backs of wooden chairs. The room was dim, lit only by the windows along one wall. Next to the windows were a few tables with dishes on them containing cakes and cookies. There were also cups and saucers and a few large teapots. At the far end of the room, standing at a lectern in front of the seated women (they were all women; I couldn't see a man anywhere) was a woman I recognized from the battle on the bandstand.

I took my hat off and held it under my arm, like Brody had shown me when I was fitted for my uniform. Annie pointed to some empty seats in the back row, and I tiptoed to them, wincing as the wooden floor creaked every time I took a step. Annie sat at my side and, for fifteen minutes, I listened to the woman talk about their struggle, and the rally taking place in Redhill on the following Saturday. At length she thanked them and stopped talking. After polite applause, most of them made a beeline for the cake and coffee (though I think only tea was on offer) while the rest crowded around the woman, all talking at once.

Annie took my hand and led me toward the knot of women at the front of the room, nodding and smiling at the few people who greeted her and gave me curious looks. When we got to the front, the knot was smaller, and Annie pushed her way inside, pulling me after her.

"Mrs. Thompson," she said.

The woman turned to her and smiled. She was taller than Annie, almost my height, wearing a lavender dress that had fewer ruffles on it than Annie's, and a matching hat that sat high on her hair, which was pulled into a tight, grey bun. "Annie," she said, "I was worried you wouldn't make it. I hope you're still planning to be at the rally. We're counting on you."

"Absolutely, Mrs. Thompson. But I'd like you to meet a friend of mine." She pulled me forward. "This is Lieutenant Wyman of the Royal Flying Corps."

Mrs. Thompson looked at me and frowned. "You're one of the young men who started the riot."

"It wasn't our fault," I said, hoping I didn't sound defensive.

"Well, I dare say it would not have happened if you and your accomplice hadn't stirred things up."

She had me there, but still, it wasn't like we'd wanted to start a fight. I was about to tell her that when Annie stepped in.

"Lieutenant Wyman has something he'd like to say about women's rights."

Mrs. Thompson cast a sceptical glance my way. "I sincerely doubt that."

"I know a great deal about it," I said, pushing my anger down, but not able to stop myself, "and I've seen many things that you can't even conceive of."

Mrs. Thompson nodded. "Love to spout off, don't you Lieutenant Wyman, just like your accomplice."

"It's Second Lieutenant," I said. "And he's not my accomplice, he's my brother."

Mrs. Thompson ignored me. "Ladies," she said to the room at large. "A government gentleman is here to shed his views on the rights of women. Please give him your attention."

I'd walked right into that, and I felt like kicking myself. Around me, expectant faces turned my way. I'd also heard the way Mrs. Thompson called me a

Government Gentleman, as if she'd wanted to spit after the words left her mouth.

"Tell them what you told me," Annie whispered.

But I couldn't. Those things were in the future. How could I convince them I knew about things if they hadn't even happened? Unless they had happened, but somewhere else, someplace they'd never heard of.

"I come from a small community in Canada," I said, looking from one face to the other. "We're isolated, with not much contact from the outside world, so we're left to get on as we see fit. And what we did, as a community, is decide that there was no need to treat women different from men."

"And what did that do?" one of the women asked. "Force women to work while men sat back and watched."

A few of the others laughed.

"No," I said. "We work together, as equals. They can vote—in local matters—they can take on any job they want, they can run for local offices. Which is why we have a woman mayor."

I heard a few gasps, so I ploughed ahead. "Women work as doctors, not just nurses. They represent men in our courtrooms. They drive cars. They deliver goods. Anything a man can do."

"And the men?" another woman asked. "What do they think about this?"

"They're fine with it," I said, realizing I had to find a way out. "We are equals. And being equal with women means everyone benefits—women, men, and children."

I stopped. The room remained silent. "That's all I have to say."

The applause started then, and my face grew hot.

"You did great," Annie whispered.

Then Mrs. Thompson was shaking my hand. "Please accept my apologies. I was certain you were just another Government agent sent to give us lip service. Your story, your words, so inspiring. You must come to the rally. Tell them what you told us here today."

"Yes, oh, yes," several nearby women chimed in.

"I'm not sure I can—"

"You must," Mrs. Thompson said. Then she turned to Annie. "You must convince him. It would make a world of difference."

Annie glanced at me. "I'll do my best."

"Oh, please do!"

We backed away from Mrs. Thompson and the admiring glances of the women.

"We probably should leave," Annie said.

"Yes," I said to the disappointed faces. "I need to return to base. I have important work to do. Flying, and all that."

Amid the nods and good-byes and Mrs. Thompson calling, "Until next Saturday," we slipped away, through the door, back down the stairs and onto the street.

I stepped in front of Annie. "How—"

"Not here," she said, glancing at the windows above us. Then she turned and marched toward the Carfax. I went after her and caught up as she rounded the corner.

"What did you think you were doing?" she asked, before I could get a word in.

"Me?" I asked. "You were the one who ordered me to perform like I was your pet dog. What did you expect me to do?" She stopped and turned to face me as I glared down at her. "And now you've got me going to your rally."

"That wouldn't have happened if you hadn't—"

"Well, that wouldn't have happened if you hadn't—"

She raised herself up on her toes until her face was level with mine and the brims of our hats knocked against one another.

"How was I supposed to know you'd make up a ridiculous story like that?"

Her eyes narrowed; her cheeks flushed red. I leaned closer, until our noses nearly touched. The words, "What was I supposed to do," ready to spring to my lips. But instead, I kissed her.

She pulled back and gasped. Then she looked around, grabbed my hand, and pulled me into a narrow gap between two building. It was strewn with trash and smelled awful, but she didn't seem to notice. When we were out of sight she turned and shoved me up against the wall.

"I don't know how things work where you're from," she shouted, her hand gripping my tie, "but we're a civilized society and we don't do that sort of thing in public."

"Sorry," I said.

"If you're going to do that, you need to go someplace no one can see you. Do you understand?"

"Yes. Yes. I told you I was sor—"

She jerked me forward, knocking both our hats off. As our lips met, she released my tie and hugged me, pulling me even closer. I wrapped my arms around her, kissing her again. And again.

Moments later, however, she pulled back, her

brow furrowed. "Did you hear that?"

I paused, listening. "No," I said, leaning in for another kiss.

She put a hand up to stop me. "Listen."

Then I heard it, a low moaning, and a rustle of papers. Deeper in the alley a pile of garbage moved, and a head appeared. It was an old man, his hair and beard matted with filth, his skin streaked with dirt. When he saw us, he pushed himself up further, as if trying to sit up. Annie gave a small squeak. "We have to leave."

"But shouldn't we help him?"

"How," she said, picking up her hat.

"Well, don't you have places for people like him to go?"

She sighed. "Yes. Jail."

I bent to retrieve my hat. "At least that would give him a place to sleep, and some food."

"It's none of our business," she said. "And he might have diseases. We really need to leave. Come on."

With that, she walked away. I watched her go, wondering if this was some sort of cultural thing, like the kissing in public. I shook my head and started after her. Then, from behind, I heard a raspy voice.

"Mitch."

I stopped, and the hairs on the back of my neck rose. Turning slowly, I saw the old man struggling to sit up. I stepped closer, nearly gagging on the stench. His clothes were nothing but tattered rags, and he clutched at them with talon-like hands as he lifted himself onto one elbow. His eyes were cloudy and dull, but in the creased skin of his face, I saw the faint line of a scar, running up his cheek, curving like a question mark around his right eye.

"Mr. Merwyn?" I asked.

"Is it you?" he croaked.

I nodded. "The Talisman, where—"

"Gone," he said, his voice laced with sadness. "Gone, and no longer believed in. Its power destroyed by the hubris of men." He drew a rasping breath and looked away. "They reject the ancient ways, they walk a path that leads to darkness, such terrifying darkness …"

I waited. He said nothing more. "What can be done?" I asked, squatting next to him.

He turned his eyes toward me. "Nothing. The Talisman can no longer save the Land. Nothing can." Then his hand shot out and grabbed mine. I struggled to not flinch. His eyes gained some of their brightness as he looked into mine. "Only you."

"Me?"

"And your bother."

"But how?"

"Follow your hearts. You know them to be steadfast and true."

From behind, I heard Annie call. "Mitch, where are you?"

"I'm going to go now," I told him. "But stay here. I'll bring help."

"You'll need your courage. All of it," he said as I pulled away. "Do not fail."

"Don't go away," I said, stepping back. "I won't be a minute."

I turned and ran down the alley, back to the Carfax, nearly colliding with Annie and a policeman. I hoped he wasn't one of the officers we had encountered during the incident.

"I've brought help," she said.

"Young lady tells me you got a vagrant on your hands," the policeman said, tapping his nightstick against the palm of his hand. "Don't fret. I'll move him along." He leered at Annie. "And you can get back to doing whatever you were doing."

Annie blushed. I glared at the cop. "There's no need, officer," I said, standing straight and making sure he noticed my lieutenant bars. "It turns out, I know him. I can take it from here."

The officer nodded slowly as he put his nightstick back in its holder. "As long as you're certain, lieutenant."

"I am. Thank you for your prompt service."

The cop took this as his cue to leave.

"Why didn't you follow me?" Annie asked. "And why did you send him away."

I took her hand and pulled her into the alley. "I wasn't lying. I know who that man is. He's the Druid."

She stopped resisting and came level with me. "Your Druid?"

"Yes, and he has a message."

We ran to where Mr. Merwyn was. Only he was no longer there. The pile of old papers, discarded ashes, and dirt had a man-shaped hole in it, but the Druid was nowhere to be seen.

I scanned the empty alley. "He can't have gone far. I was gone only a few seconds."

Annie looked one way, then the other. "There's no way out, and he didn't go past us. Are you sure you saw him?"

"Of course I saw him. So did you."

"I did see something. A man, certainly, but I don't

142

know that he was a Druid."

"Well, I am. I spoke to him. And he told me things," I said, suddenly feeling the weight of his words.

Annie looked at me, concerned. "What things?"

"That the Talisman is gone. That there is no hope."

She made a sound between a hiccup and a sob. "None?"

"He said it was up to me to save the Land. Me and Charlie. But we won't have the Talisman to help us."

Annie smiled. "If you're the one to save us, then there is hope. And I'll help."

"I need to get back to the base."

"What? Now? We have all day—"

"I need to talk to Charlie," I said, ignoring the disappointment on her face. "Can you get me a ticket. I'll take the train and get a cab."

"I'll come with you."

"There's no need for that. I can find my way—"

"Listen, mate," she said, leaning toward me, her lips inches from mine. "You can sit on the train by yourself brooding over your Druid, or we can sit together in a private compartment, kissing. Which would you prefer?"

The choice was obvious.

Chapter 20

Charlie

Shooting the Lewis gun was fun, even though I was—as Newell noted—a bit rubbish at it.

Before he allowed me to touch the gun, Newell schooled me on all the ins and outs, showing me how to load the pans, or drum magazines, in the most efficient manner, how to securely attach the drum to the gun, and how to position myself for firing.

Having seen the Lewis gun in action several times now, I had come to realize it wasn't as large, or fearsome, as I had first thought. It looked like a big rifle with a really long tin can for a barrel. Newell told me that was to keep the barrel cool. I attached the drum like he had shown me, laid down, put the stock snuggly against my shoulder and slid the bolt back to load the first shell.

"Short bursts," he said. "You don't want to overheat the barrel. Take aim, steady yourself and pull the trigger back for a second, then release. Got it?"

I nodded, sighted in on the nearest target, and pulled the trigger. The familiar tat-tat-tat I'd heard in countless war movies was magnified a million times. The gun roared and rattled and jumped around. I struggled to hold it steady, to keep the spray of bullets on the target, but they weren't going anywhere near it. By the time I had the gun almost under control, the rattling stopped. I looked at the smoking barrel and realized my finger was still holding the trigger; I had emptied the entire pan.

Newell chuckled. "Not bad for a first try. Load up another magazine, and let the barrel cool a bit."

I loaded two pans, both to give the Lewis gun a chance to recover, and to see how efficiently, and quickly, I could do it. That part, at least, I was getting better at, but when I attached the first pan to the gun and pulled the trigger, I still couldn't hit anything. This time, however, I was able to keep the Lewis gun under control and fire in short bursts.

"You're getting better," Newell observed, "but it is going to take some time."

Fortunately, time seemed to be something we had a lot of. With the necessary chemicals still in the supply chain, Major Billings and Captain Jeffreys spent their time devising and refining formulas and Farber kept busy by going into town. So, Captain Newell and I were left to waste as many bullets as we wanted.

I did get better after a while, but not before Newell had to retrieve another box of ammo (I say box, but it was more like a case). In the early afternoon, Newell had me make a batch of my own bullets, both normal ammunition, and some of the Buckingham bullets with the old formulas. He seemed impressed with how I handled that, and when I used new bullets on the firing range, I was able to hit the nearest, and second nearest, target.

"You are showing remarkable improvement," Newell said after I emptied the second drum. "But it would serve you well to keep at it. You'll have ample free time until the proper chemicals arrive, and you know where this gun, and the ammunition, is kept." He fished in his pocket, pulled out a ring with two keys on it, and pointed to the smaller one. "This is for the ammunition store. Be sure to note what you have taken in the book."

I nodded. "Yes, Sir."

"This other one is for the lab. You know where the Lewis gun is. You are free to take it whenever you have free time and wish to practice."

I couldn't hide my surprise. "Yes, Sir."

"You will, of course, thoroughly clean the weapon before you put it away."

"Um, yes, sir," I said, a little less confidently.

"If you need some assistance with that, sergeant, come and find me."

"Thank you, sir. Yes, sir. I will, sir."

Newell grinned. "You'll make a fine soldier one day. Just keep practicing, and learn to say LEF tenant."

I was tired of saying "Sir," so I merely nodded.

Newell turned to leave, but then stopped. "Sergeant. Most importantly, when you do go to the lab to retrieve or return the Lewis gun, if I am not around, be sure you obtain permission from Major Billings. You do not yet have a proper security clearance and the major doesn't like unauthorized personnel poking about in top secret facilities."

"Understood, sir."

And then he left me alone with the Lewis gun. I loaded, and shot off, a few more drums, pleased to see I was getting better at both. After a short time, however, I decided I'd done enough. I had seen Newell enter the lab earlier, and I wanted to get the Lewis gun back before he left so he could show me how to clean it because I didn't have the faintest idea.

As I picked up the brass, I saw Mitch running my way, still wearing his ridiculous uniform.

"Back so soon?" I asked, as he drew near.

"I saw him," Mitch said, gasping. "Mr. Merwyn, Malcolm, the Druid."

"Here? He's here?"

A nod. Then he stopped a few feet away.

"What did he want? What did he say?"

Mitch shook his head and looked at the ground. An icy chill formed in my chest.

"What is it?"

"He hasn't found the Talisman. It's gone. Lost. And no one believes in it, anyway." He looked up. "He says there is no hope. There's only us."

"But we brought the bullet."

"There's more, I think. He gave me the feeling that delivering the bullet wasn't enough."

"What else can we do? They've got the new formula now."

I thought about what I had learned that morning, and that I couldn't tell him.

When I didn't say anything, Charlie asked, "Where is he?"

"That's just it. He disappeared. He said those few words, I turned away, and when I turned back, he was gone."

"So, we're on our own."

Mitch sighed. "I believe so."

I looked beyond Mitch. We wouldn't be on our own for long. Brody was approaching from the direction of the hangar, and Major Billings was coming from the Lab. They reached us at the same time.

"Lieutenant Huntington," Billings said.

"Major Billings," Brody said, raising his hand in a salute. "I've come to take Lieutenant Wyman up for a lesson. I see he has returned earlier than expected, and there is plenty of daylight left."

"Second Lieutenant," Billings said, then he looked at Mitch. "Yes, you have returned early. Is my niece well?"

"She's fine, Major Billings," Mitch said, saluting. "I simply returned early."

Billings grunted and looked at me. "Captain Newell informs me you are now proficient in the making of bullets."

"Uh, yes, sir. He trained me to use his, um, apparatus, and Captain Farber's."

"I see," he said, looking at Brody. "That makes you more valuable to me than a mere sergeant. So, I am hereby promoting you to Lieutenant." He turned to Mitch. "First Lieutenant Wyman. Visit the quartermaster at your earliest opportunity and acquire the proper uniform."

Brody scowled. "Second Lieutenant Wyman, with me."

And then I was alone. I sighed and went back to picking up the brass, because that was better than dwelling on what Mitch had just told me.

Chapter 21
Wednesday, 30 August 1916

Mitch

Dear Annie,

A lot has happened since I saw you. Remember how I told you that Brody had said he was going to teach me to fly? Well, on Sunday, after I left you and told Charlie about what Mr. Merwyn had said, Brody found me and took me to the hangar, which is what they call the shed they keep the airplanes in. Brody showed me how to do a preflight check. That was pretty cool, and a lot easier than I imagined. There are so few parts on these planes and most of them are really simple. Just wires and levers and, as long as everything is connected, it all works fine. The most complicated thing is the engine, but all you need to do is fill it with oil and petrol and you're on your way. The worst thing about the engine is starting it. You have to push the propeller around by hand. It's hard, and dangerous but, fortunately, I don't have to do that.

The airplanes I'm used to are solid, and made of metal, but the ones here are just a wooden frame with material stretched over it. At first, I thought they were really flimsy, but they are stronger than they look. They are light, though. Brody and I pushed his plane out of the hangar by ourselves. Whittard and Moore helped us get it ready, brought us our flying gear, and started the engine.

Brody had me watch while he worked all the controls to show me what they did. Then he told me to get into the observer's seat and strap in. Brody's method of training was to shout what he was doing as we took off. It was hard to hear him, but I think I got most of it. The airplane's controls, just like the airplane itself, are pretty simple. There's a speedometer that shows how fast you are going, but it's in knots, which I don't understand very well, and there's an altimeter that shows how high you are, which, fortunately, is in feet. There's also a compass to tell you which direction you are flying, and a thing that tells you if the airplane is level or tilting or upside down. Aside from that, there are some pressure gauges and RPM dials, but Brody says I don't have to worry about them unless they go into the red zone.

There's no steering wheel in the plane. You control it with pedals and a stick that's bolted to the floor. Brody tells me there are wires attached that control the rudders and elevators. While on the ground, he had me work with them, and told me to watch what they did.

The airplane bounces terribly when it's on the ground, but it doesn't take long to get airborne, and then it's as smooth as silk.

Flying is brilliant. When he took me up, I felt so free and light. The weather, though warm on the ground, turned cold up in the air. Brody showed me how to fly level, climb and dive. Then he took it in for a landing, telling me to watch carefully.

He shouted out what he was doing as the plane levelled, angled toward the field, and thumped to the ground. As we taxied toward the hangar, I saw Whittard and Moore pulling the other plane onto the grass, and Brody pulled up next to it.

Both planes are SE3c models. The one Brody uses is a standard design. He calls it Mrs. Beeton, and it's what he transports the ammunition to the other bases in. The second airplane is what Whittard and Moore call their Night Fighter, because that's what it's designed for. It's used mostly for observation, though, so that's what Brody calls it: the Observation Plane. It's kept on base as a backup. Mostly, though, it sits in the hangar.

Since we're a research base and not a fighting base, however, Whittard and Moore have been allowed to make some modifications to it. First of all, they painted it black so it can't be easily seen at night. This seemed so obvious, but they reminded me that paint adds weight. Standard Night Fighters don't have a second seat, as that space is taken up with an extra fuel tank to enable them to fly longer, so they have time to get up to where the Zeppelins are. Whittard and Moore moved the tank and restored the observer's seat, outfitting it with a duplicate set of controls as well as a bracket for a Lewis gun. To counter the weight issues these modifications presented, they remodelled the engine, fuselage, and landing gear to lighten the plane, making it more manoeuvrable, faster, and fuel efficient. These changes not only allow the pilot to concentrate on flying while the gunner concentrates on shooting, which makes a lot of sense, but also means the gunner, if trained properly, can bring the plane down safely if the pilot is injured. Or killed.

It also makes it ideal for training pilots.

And so, as the sun sank low, we went up a second time. In the Observer plane, the pilot sits up front, so I was in the back seat with the duplicate controls. I wasn't allowed to take off, but Brody told me to keep my hands lightly on the control stick to get a feel for it. Once in the air, Brody held his arms up to show he was no longer controlling the airplane, and it was up to me. Incredibly, I wasn't scared, or even nervous. It felt natural, and the plane responded as I eased the stick and pressed the pedals. I flew around for quite a while, with Brody pointing out landmarks from the pilot's seat.

After an hour or so, he told me to head back to base, using the landmarks he had pointed out, and gauging our position by the compass and the glow in the west where the sun had gone down. Once again, I found it exhilarating, though a little harder as the land became darkened by shadow. Eventually, I recognized Redhill, and then Earlswood and turned toward where the sun had been to head for the base.

Brody landed, naturally, but I kept my hands on the controls and my eyes on the wings.

It was nearly dark by the time we got down, which gave me a chance to see another innovation of Whittard and Moore. They had rigged up a light to illuminate the instruments, making night flight a lot easier. As we bounced and rolled toward the hangar I was already looking forward to the next lesson.

After the flight, and after helping Whittard and Moore check over the planes, I asked why the other bases weren't adopting their designs. They admitted that, even after all their modifications, the airplane weighed more than the current model, which meant it had less time in the air. And they were having trouble convincing anyone that the advantage of the gunner outweighed the loss of flight time. Then they asked if I could put in a word for them.

I wondered why they thought I had that ability, and I felt bad when I told them I would see what I could do because I knew I couldn't do anything and that I would end up disappointing them.

But there's not a lot I can do about that, and I have my own problems, mainly that I'm stuck here without you, and I really, really miss you and I am so looking forward to seeing you again.

I almost forgot: Charlie has been promoted to First Lieutenant. When Brody found me, Charlie was with your Uncle Henry, and he noted that Charlie had learned enough about how to make the bullets to become an officer. So, he promoted him to a rank just above me. Funny thing, though. I don't think it was for Charlie's benefit. He was looking at Brody, and me, when he did it.

Keep safe, and well.

Love,
Mitch

MEMORANDUM

TO: Major Billings
From: Sergeant Dobson
Subject: Censored Communication

The attached letter cannot possibly leave this base. Ninety percent of it will need to be redacted. What is quite remarkable is that this "officer" seems to have no knowledge (or regard?) for military protocol, or secrecy. I would recommend the destruction of this letter, and the termination of the author's rank.

MEMORANDUM

TO: Sergeant Dobson
From: Major Billings
Subject: Censored Communication

Good work, Sergeant Dobson. Send the revised (attached) letter to my niece, and tell Second Lieutenant Wyman and Lieutenant Huntington to see me immediately.

And find out what Whittard and Moore are doing with that blasted airplane.

ATTACHMENT

Dear Annie,
A lot has happened since I saw you.
XXXXXXXXXXXX XXXX XXXXX XXXXXX
XXX XXXXXXXXXXXX XXX XXXX XX XXX
XXX XXXXXXX XXXXXXXX XXX XXX XXX
XXXXXXX XX XXXXXX XX X XXXXX XX
XXX XXXXXXX XXXX XX XXX XXX XXXX
XX.

XXX XXXXXXXXXXXX XXX XXXX XX
XXX XXX XXXXXXX XXXXXXXX XXX XXX
XXX XXXXXXX XX XXXXXX XX X XXXXX
XX XXX XXXXXXX XXXX XX XXX XXX
XXXX XX XXXX.

XXX XXXXXXXXXXXX XXX XXXX XX
XXX XXX XXXXXXX XXXXXXXX XXX XXX
XXX XXXXXXX XX XXXXXX XX X XXXXX
XX XXX XXXXXXX XXXX XX XXX XXX
XXXX.

XXXXXX XX XXXXXXXX XXX XXX XX XX
XXX XX XXXXXX XXX.

Charlie has been promoted to First Lieutenant.

XXXX,
Mitch

Chapter 22
Friday, 1 September 1916

Charlie

Production on the new bullets didn't start until Friday. This was due to the order being delayed, and then the chemicals were sent to the wrong base. This is typical of the army, but it made everyone nervous. A Zeppelin raid could come at any time, and every night, Major Billings and the other officers, which now included me, sat around a radio in his office, listening to reports and dreading the news that more Zeppelins were on the way.

Fortunately, none came. And on Thursday afternoon the necessary chemicals arrived, but that didn't end the agony. Captain Jeffreys spent hours mixing the new formula and, just as it was getting dark, we were able to make a few dozen bullets and rush them out to the firing range to test them. This time, I was the one on the Lewis gun, but I had been practicing all week, so even with the others watching, I wasn't nervous, and managed to hit the target even though it was four hundred yards away.

The trace burned the whole way, lighting the darkening field like a speedy firefly. After shooting half the bullets, Major Billings called a halt to the test and ordered us all back to the lab. While I cleaned and stowed the Lewis gun, Billings locked the remaining bullets in a small safe.

"Tomorrow, first thing, we re-test those bullets," he said. "Until then, you are all to stand down." When Newell and Jeffreys began to protest, Billings raised his hand to silence them. "We can't deliver any bullets tonight, anyway, and we cannot afford to send duff rounds to the pilots again. If these bullets don't degrade overnight, like the previous batch, we'll make more. Lieutenant Huntington will deliver them and, God willing, by this time tomorrow, all the bases will be armed with the ammunition they need to bring down a Zeppelin."

"What about tonight?" Jeffreys asked.

Billings sighed. "God has smiled upon us every night this week. We have to hope His grace will see us through another. We will monitor in my office, as usual."

"I'm going to assume the new formula is stable," Jeffreys said. "I'll stay here and mix more. That way, as soon as the test is complete, production can begin. We haven't any time to lose."

Billings nodded. "Good plan. Do what you can, then meet us in my office."

We left Captain Jeffreys in the lab and assembled in the Major's office where we spent another night huddled around the radio, drinking bitter coffee and praying no Zeppelins were spotted. It had been a nerve-wracking exercise all week, but this was worse because we were so close to success. Near midnight, Jeffreys arrived, looking bleary eyed but triumphant.

"Good news?" he asked, as he entered.

"No news," Billings said, not taking his eyes off the radio.

Jeffreys nodded. "I've mixed a batch that can fill

thousands of bullets. We'll need to work fast tomorrow." He looked at Billings. "After the test, of course."

Then he sat down, drank a cup of cold coffee, and waited along with the rest of us.

At one o'clock, Farber left. At two o'clock, Billings said that if they hadn't come by then, they weren't going to. So, relieved, we went to our rooms.

Since my unexpected promotion, my quarters had been upgraded. Not much, but I had been moved to a larger room, one with a big cabinet in it that they called a wardrobe, which contained several new uniforms. Other than that, there wasn't much difference, aside from Sergeant Dobson bringing me tea and laying out my clothes at five thirty in the morning. I felt embarrassed and asked him to not keep doing it, but he told me that was his job and, as an officer, I got that service whether I liked it or not, which made me wonder what good being an officer was if I couldn't tell people what to do.

On the plus side, my bed was bigger and more comfortable, and I had my own bathroom. I also got to eat with the officers, so me and Mitch were now at the same table, where Lieutenant Huntington glared at Major Billings, and Billings glared at Second Lieutenant Mitch, and I kept my head down.

Another good outcome was none of the soldiers bothered me when I practiced with the Lewis gun, which, since we didn't have a lot to do that week, was a lot. I'd go out early, get the Lewis gun and a case of ammo, and just shoot. It was surprisingly relaxing, but it made my ears ring. So, after rattling off half a dozen drums, I searched through the ammo store and the lab looking for ear defenders. There were some extra lab coats, rubber gloves, gas masks, and a few pair of heavy work boots, but that was all. When I asked Newell if they had any lying around I could borrow, he didn't know what I was talking about. And when I explained it to him, he became even more mystified.

"Why would you want something like that?" he asked. "In battle, they'd never fit under your helmet, and in an airplane, the wind would rip them off your head."

I thought about telling him I didn't expect either of those things to happen, and if they did, I'd rather not have to do them deaf, but instead I just found some cotton and stuffed that in my ears. And, as an officer, none of the soldiers patrolling around the grounds while I practiced dared laugh, at least not to my face.

By the time Friday morning finally arrived, I felt proficient enough with the Lewis gun that I didn't mind the four of them standing over me while I loaded the test bullets. There were only six of them, so I didn't use the drum magazine. I just pulled the bolt back, loaded them one at a time, aimed at the far target, and fired. The hardest part was not fist-pumping the air and shouting "Yes!" when I bulls-eyed it.

"The trace lasted the entire length of the field, and beyond," Jeffreys said, with a hint of I-told-you-so in his voice.

Billings shook his head. "I want to test the mixture you made last night, just to be sure. It's been sitting in the lab for over twelve hours. We don't know how long it takes for it to degrade."

"If it degrades," Jeffreys said. "There is no reason to—"

"I have some here," Captain Farber said, holding up three bullets. "I thought it best to be safe, so I made these just after breakfast." He glanced at Captain Newell, who looked surprised. "I didn't think you'd mind me invading your workstation. You were otherwise engaged and time, as we know, is critical."

Billings nodded. "Good man. Test these rounds, Lieutenant Wyman."

I loaded one of the bullets into the Lewis gun and fired. It worked as well as the others, and I hit the target in the same place.

"Good shot," Billings said.

"Are you satisfied now, sir?" Jeffreys said, a brittle edge to his voice.

Production began at ten o'clock, at a pace we had never worked at before. A real factory could have turned out tens of thousands of rounds in the time we had available to us, but Major Billings wouldn't release the formula until he was "one hundred and ten percent" certain it was viable. And so, we worked as fast and efficiently as we could, and soon found that Farber could fill slugs a lot faster than Newell could load charges, so they scouted up a second machine, one that looked cobbled together and was probably what they used while they were trying to fix the one Sergeant Rutherford had blown up. Fortunately, Newell used that one, leaving the one I was used to for me.

After that, for the rest of the day, it was press, press, press. Then, when the bullets piled up, I loaded as many drums as I could and brought them out to Brody, who—along with Mitch—flew them to the bases. This assembly line ran for eight solid hours until, near six o'clock, Billings called a halt. By then, we had filled thousands of Buckingham bullets and sent hundreds of fully loaded magazines to every air base in our vicinity. After taking the final load to Brody, I returned to a tired but satisfied team.

"That's enough for today," Billings told us. "We're nearly out of materials, the pilots have enough ammunition to bring down a hundred Zeppelins, and Lieutenant Huntington is on his last run."

"I've made a final batch with the last of the chemicals," Jeffreys said. "Enough for about two thousand rounds."

Billings nodded. "That will keep. We'll make the rest on Monday and, after a few more tests, I'll notify the War Office. But for now, we've done enough. It's time to celebrate." Then he looked at me. "And it's a double celebration for you, Lieutenant Wyman."

"Sir?"

"You have proved yourself fit to be a full member of this team, so I'm hereby promoting you. Congratulations, Captain Wyman."

"Um, thank you, Sir," I said, stunned. "Are you sure?"

Billings smiled and turned away. "As certain as Lieutenant Huntington is."

We retired to a small, private dining room, with a table set for the five of us. Dinner was brought in—beef, lots of it, and potatoes with gravy—then dessert, a mash-up of berries and cream, and, finally, beer and whiskey.

As darkness fell, the table was cleared—but the beer and whiskey were left—and Billings had the radio brought in. We sat around it, listening as we had every night that week, only this time we were hoping for an attack. If one came, the pilots were as prepared as they could be to meet it. And if they failed, the blame would fall on them, not us, which seemed to be the point of the whole exercise.

I stuck with beer and sipped it slowly, but even so, felt myself fading after an hour or so. I hung on grimly, dreading our celebration turning into an obligatory, all-night session until, around eleven o'clock, Farber announced he was heading to his quarters for some much-needed sleep. No one called him a pussy after he left, so I thought it was safe to do the same, making it back to my warm—and only slightly spinning—bed just before midnight.

I was sinking into the mattress, content to sleep in my uniform, when I began thinking about what Mitch had told me. The Druid, if not dead, was at least powerless to help. It was, according to Mitch, up to us, and we didn't even have the Talisman. All we had was what we'd brought with us: the cloak, which was currently out of reach, and the bullet, which was empty.

Should I fill it? I could have easily done that during the day, and I could still do it sometime tomorrow, but a sudden sense of urgency gripped me, pulling me, reluctantly, out of bed. It would be a simple thing to do, and I was certainly competent enough. All I needed was permission. But when I approached the dining room, I found they were quite drunk, so I decided to not bother them. Instead, I found a flashlight and went out into the night, avoiding, as much as possible, the sentries and security patrols.

At the lab, I unlocked the door, stepped into the darkness, and locked it behind me. Only then did I turn on the flashlight. It was a primitive thing they called a torch, which was appropriate because the beam was almost as useful as a burning stick, but at least it wouldn't draw attention the way turning on all the lights would.

I made my way to Farber's station. The glass beaker filled with the new formula sat near the end of his workbench. It was the final batch Captain Jeffreys had made that afternoon, sealed in the glass container by a large cork, ready to be put into more bullets. Carefully, I eased the cover off the beaker and used the scoop to pour the proper amount into Farber's machine. Then I placed our bullet's slug in the device and squeezed the powder into it. After I was done, I cleaned the tools and the machine, put the cork back in the beaker and set it back where I had found it.

Then I headed toward Captain Newell's work area where I planned to crimp the two parts together. Once that was done, it would be just like it had been when we had arrived. I was nearly there when I heard the door open and close.

Then the lights came on.

Chapter 23

Mitch

Dear Annie,

It's late and I know I'm seeing you tomorrow, but I really want to tell you about my day, and this is the only way I can do it. Writing with pencil and paper feels strange to me. Remind me to tell you about email and Skype when I see you.

Thanks for your letter. I keep it in my breast pocket, and I've already read it about twenty times. Sorry to hear mine was so disappointing.

I'll be handing this letter to you in person tomorrow because that will be safer than mailing it. I got into so much trouble sending the last one. Your Uncle called me and Brody into his office and (as Brody noted later) read me the riot act. Apparently, what I put in that letter was top secret, and he was all, who do I think I am, and what did I think I was playing at, and did I know how much danger I was putting everyone in, and I think he would have demoted me if Brody hadn't been there.

I don't know what you were able to read in that letter, but even more amazing things have happened since. Spoiler alert: Brody promoted me to first lieutenant. Your uncle said he couldn't do that because he, himself, was a first lieutenant but Brody said he saw no reason not to, as he'd be the more senior lieutenant and, therefore, my superior. Your uncle wasn't happy about that, so he promoted Charlie to captain. If their feud carries on much longer, we'll both be generals by October.

Anyway, during the week, Brody had been taking me up to fly as often as he could and using the Observation plane to teach me how to operate the airplane myself. I learned how to take off yesterday, and today Brody let me land, without any practice.

But I'm getting ahead of myself. Here's what's been happening:

The chemicals needed to make the bullets finally arrived, and this morning production started in earnest and, all afternoon, Charlie kept bringing filled pan magazines to Brody for delivery to the other bases. He took me with him, in the Observer plane, so I could practice, and in the late afternoon he let me take off from one of the bases that had a hard runway. He said it would be easier with the plane not bouncing around like it did on the grassy field our base uses. Still, I was stunned, thinking I was nowhere near ready, but he shouted instructions to me as I taxied the airplane onto the runway and revved up the engine. As we moved along the tarmac, the airplane gained speed and, suddenly, we were in the air.

I was so surprised I laughed. Then Brody told me that was the easy bit; landing was harder.

We spent all day flying from one base to the other, and although Charlie brought the ammunition to me, we didn't get to talk because we were all so busy: him making bullets, Brody and me flying them to the bases, and Whittard and Moore preparing the airplane between runs.

When the final batch was delivered to us early this

evening, Brody told me he wanted us to fly them to RAF Hornchurch—which the guys call Sutton's Farm—using Mrs. Beeton, with me piloting and Brody sitting in the observer's seat.

I thought he was joking, but as Whittard and Moore prepared the airplane, he got into the observer's seat and started giving me instructions on what to do and how to do it. So, I climbed into the cockpit, Whittard spun the propeller, Brody shouted instructions, and I taxied the airplane onto the field and revved up the engine. I'd already done one take-off, but this one was harder. We bounced along the ground as the airplane rolled forward, gaining speed and jostling at a frightening rate, until I eased the joystick back and took us into the darkening sky.

I recognized the towns of Reigate and Redhill, and soon we were on the outskirts of London, which is easy to recognize because it stretches for miles and miles. As the sun sank lower and shadows covered the ground, it became difficult to navigate by sight, and I had to rely on my compass and speedometer. Brody helped a little, and a short while after crossing the Thames, I spotted an airfield just ahead and to the right of us.

It's harder than you think to recognize places from the air. To me it looked like a big farm, which I suppose it was, but one side of it had a brown stripe on the ground that Brody told me was the landing strip. It was bigger than our base and, as we got closer, I could see hangars and barracks and men and airplanes and a few trucks. I eased down toward the base, following Brody's instructions about turning the plane to face the landing strip and making sure I lined up straight. He told me to aim for a spot in front of the runway for me to touch down on. I thought he was crazy, but it turned out I was so nervous I was still twenty feet in the air when I got to it, which I'm sure Brody knew I would be. As I passed it, he told me to keep easing the plane down, and down, and down.

Then we bounced onto the hard packed earth, which was smooth and flat, making it easier to keep the plane under control than when it's bouncing over the grass. As I taxied up to one of the hangars, airmen and a few officers came out to greet us, offering a flask of whiskey as soon as our feet hit the ground. Brody took a swig, lit his pipe, and started shaking hands and slapping airmen on the back. Then he introduced me and told them I was the most natural pilot he had ever seen. So, the whiskey flask was shoved into my hands, and I had to take a swig and not choke as the others shook my hand and slapped my back.

Then another Airman came toward us. He was of average height, with dark hair and a small moustache, but he carried himself in a way that made you take notice. He walked up to us smiling, and slapped Brody on the back. Brody whacked him back and they began talking about their Oxford days and we wandered away from the others who were busy distributing the pans.

The other Airman, who Brody introduced as Lieutenant William Leefe-Robinson, led us to one of the hangars and pointed to his airplane. It was a standard BE2c Night Fighter, but there was a big, fancy design, in bright red, painted on the sides. He told Brody it was his family crest and he had talked his commander into allowing it so the Huns would know who was shooting at them. They both laughed at that as if it was some sort of hilarious joke, so I joined in.

Brody then got serious and told the Lieutenant about the new bullets and instructed him to shoot the exploding Brock and Pomeroy bullets into one area, then to shoot the Buckingham bullets into the same area. He told him that would certainly show the Hun who was boss and then they slapped each other on the backs again.

After that, we went back to our airplane, which was prepared and waiting for us near the landing strip. Brody took the pilot seat because the evening was drawing in and it wouldn't be easy to find our base in the dark. I was happy to leave it to him, so I climbed into the observer's seat and waved, and we took off. I spent the return trip pretending I was flying, and thinking how I would navigate, but I soon became confused.

Back at base, we found the other officers celebrating, so we celebrated on our own, sitting with Whittard and Moore around a barrel they'd built a fire in. Brody smoked his pipe, congratulated me on my promotion—even though, by then, he had heard about Charlie's—and we passed a bottle of whiskey around. We knew that the others were being served dinner in a private dining room, but we didn't care. They had done an amazing job, but we had faced a more difficult, and dangerous challenge (though not as dangerous as the fighter pilots would face when the Zeppelins came) and that made us brothers in arms. There was no distinction of rank or social status, and the camaraderie infected me, in a good way, and put me so at ease that I wasn't even worried about the rally tomorrow, or what I'm going to say when I'm called on to speak.

It's late at night now. I expect Charlie is still up, celebrating with his buddies, but I'm ready for bed. I've got a big day tomorrow, and I'm counting the minutes until I'm with you again. I will be up and out early, on my way to the rally, and expect to be there well before noon.

See you then.

Love,

Mitch

Chapter 24
Saturday, 2 September 1916

Charlie

I dropped to the floor and turned off the torch. No one shouted or called for me to show myself, so I was pretty sure whoever it was hadn't seen me. I crept by inches to Captain Newell's station and hid behind a cabinet as footsteps came closer.

Carefully, I peeked out and saw Farber at his workbench. My stomach dropped. Had I cleaned up properly? He was so OCD he'd know if someone had been there. I held my breath and waited.

Farber didn't seem to notice anything amiss, however. He fished around on the nearby shelves for a large glass bowl, then opened the beaker containing the mixture and dumped it in. From inside his jacket, he pulled out a test tube and emptied white powder into the bowl. I shifted to get a better look, bumped an ammunition rack, and almost gasped out loud. It wobbled but I grabbed it to keep it from falling. Farber stopped. I ducked and waited. No footsteps. I counted to fifty and took another peek.

He was stirring the powder mixture with a stick, and not being very careful. It spread over the workbench, and some of it even fell onto the floor. When it was all blended together, he carefully poured the new mixture into the beaker and put the stopper back on. Then he spent a long time cleaning up his workbench, so it looked as if nothing had happened.

After taking a last look around, he walked silently to the door, turned off the lights and slipped out.

I stayed where I was, taking slow, deep breaths, listening to see if he was trying to fool me and was still inside. I counted to three hundred. No sound. I stood up and turned on the torch. I was alone.

Farber coming to the lab on his own, even this late at night, wasn't something out of the ordinary. They all worked strange hours, and Captain Jeffreys and Major Billings were always rushing to the lab to try out their latest inspiration, but this seemed different. He hadn't been nervous, but he had been sneaky. And just what had he been doing?

I went to his workbench. It looked the same as it had when I left it. The beaker stood exactly where Jeffreys had put it, the workbench was clean, and all the powder—even what he had spilled on the floor— had been swept away. Nothing was wrong, except that Farber had added something to the mixture. He was a technician, not a chemist, so there was no reason for him to do that, unless he was making sure the new formula didn't work.

I looked at our bullet. If I was right about what Farber was doing, it might be the only good bullet we had. And if it was to be a good bullet, it needed to be a proper bullet. I went back to Captain Newell's area and, without hesitation, filled the casing with cordite and sealed it.

Now all I needed to do was figure out how to tell Captain Newell, Captain Jeffreys and Major Billings about Farber without telling them what I'd done myself. The answer turned out to be simple: they already thought I might be a Government agent from the War Office. I'd could capitalize on that. The real problem was how I was going to tell them anything at all.

I slipped out of the lab and hurried back to the dining room. As I suspected, they were still there, holding up the ragged end of their long celebration. Unannounced, I walked in and sat at the table.

Newell raised his glass. "Captain Wyman," he said, his bleary eyes brightening, "welcome back. Have you returned to inject new life into our flagging festivities?"

I shook my head. "I'm afraid not." They looked at me expectantly and I thought the kindest thing to do would be to tell them outright. "I didn't leave to go to my bunk. I left to follow Farber. He went to the lab." I looked at Jeffreys. "He mixed something into your formula. I believe he is sabotaging us."

They all stared at me and set their glasses on the table. As I told them more about what I had seen, they pushed them further away, and seemed to sober up.

"Where is he now?" Billings asked when I had finished.

"In his room."

Jeffreys nodded. "We need to arrest him. Now."

"No," Billings said, fastening the top button on his uniform and straightening his tie. "We need to find out what he did. Quietly, and without raising suspicions."

After a short argument about how we should do that, we left for the lab. The four of us heading there, even at that late hour, wouldn't be remarkable, and Farber, we hoped, would be asleep.

At Farber's workstation, Jeffreys inspected the mixture.

"It doesn't look any different," he said, "but that means nothing. We need to test it."

He put a small scoop on a metal plate and took it to the far end of Farber's station, away from anything flammable. There, he touched a match to it. A small flame shot up, sputtered, and died.

"It's behaving the same as the first batch," Jeffreys said. "The one we thought had degraded."

I gave him credit for not pointing out that Billings was the one who insisted it had degraded, but I guess he wasn't in the mood for scoring points.

Newell, his face white, said, "What about the bullets we made today?"

Billings frowned. "Are there any that we can test?"

"A few," I said. "We didn't have enough bullets to fill the last drum. I left it on the table near the Lewis guns."

We went to the table at the far corner of the lab, me walking a bit straighter and faster than the others. When I got there, I slid a few bullets out of the magazine and held one up. "This is one we made this afternoon," I said. "But how are we going to test it without making a lot of noise."

Newell had obviously thought about this, because he had grabbed a pair of pliers along the way.

He pried the slug off, while I winced and waited for it to explode, then used a nail to scrape the incendiary mixture onto the table. He didn't bother putting it on a metal plate, he just struck a match and touched it to the powder. It didn't flare up like it should have. Instead, it sputtered and smoked, and left a scorch-mark on the tabletop.

Newell turned and looked at Billings. "All the drums we delivered to the bases, all the slugs we filled, all the bullets we charged, all eight thousand, five hundred and sixty-three of them, are useless."

Chapter 25

Mitch

On Saturday, I was up early and ate alone in the Officer's Mess while everyone else was sleeping off the previous night's celebrations. The Captains and Uncle Henry were nowhere to be seen, Brody hadn't stirred, and Charlie was undoubtedly still lounging in his new Captain's quarters.

Outside, the morning was fresh, the clouds were high and the sun, though bright, remained hidden behind the trees. It was going to be a good day for the rally. It wasn't due to start until four in the afternoon, and my part wasn't until nearly seven (which I preferred to not think about), but the sooner I got there, the sooner I'd be with Annie, so I started out as early as possible.

My pass was for the whole day—from dawn until midnight—so I set off right after breakfast. The only way I could get into town was walk (Uncle Henry was reluctant enough to give me the pass, so I doubted he'd have thrown in a lift to the station) but it wasn't that far, and Annie had given me directions so I couldn't get lost even though I was going to Redhill, where I had never been before. I'd seen it from the air a number of times, but that was different.

Captain Farber was at the entrance, talking to Corporal Blake. I saluted, like I was supposed to, but he ignored me while Blake gave my pass a cursory glance and pushed the gate open far enough to allow me to slip through. I resisted the urge to say "Thanks" because I didn't think that was how officers acted with enlisted men, and then I realized that, although I had saluted Captain Farber, Blake had not saluted me. I could have made an issue of it but, instead, I left them and the base behind, headed toward town, and concentrated on enjoying the solitude and the clear, crisp morning.

September had only just arrived, and although the trees were leafy and green and the sun shone through the canopy in a summer-like dazzle of bright and dark, the scent of autumn was in the air, making me slightly homesick and longing to see Annie. I sank so deep into reverie that I didn't notice the time go by, or the car fast approaching from behind. I jumped aside just in time to see what looked like a Model-T, painted a military khaki colour, rattle past. Captain Farber was driving, and I had the unsettling feeling he would have happily run me over if I hadn't moved.

I was still marvelling at this when I heard another vehicle, so I stepped further onto the verge and turned to see who was trying to run me down this time. It was a truck, an army truck, with Sergeant Orr driving and Sergeant Dobson next to him. I waved, but they zoomed by without even acknowledging me, or stopping to offer me a lift.

My irritation lasted only a few seconds. They were likely on a mission of some sort, and picking up hitchhikers wasn't part of it, even if the hitchhiker was a full Lieutenant. Besides, walking in the dappled sunshine was nicer than bouncing over the rutted road in an ancient automobile.

I made it to Earlswood in just over an hour. I was supposed to catch the train to Redhill there, but it was still early, and my destination was only a mile or two away, so I walked, following the Brighton Road along the cluster of houses that was Earlswood until it merged with the larger cluster of houses and factories that was Redhill. As I passed a massive collection of brick buildings, steel structures, and huge iron pipes that—on the largest building, in ten-foot-high white lettering—proclaimed itself to be the gasworks, the road name changed to Redhill High Street, which was the street I was looking for. The sports ground, where the rally was taking place, was on the far side of Redhill, but it didn't take long to get there, and it wasn't hard to find.

About two hundred yards past the road that led to Redhill Station, I saw a large green area, bordered by a low, wrought iron fence, on the right side of the road. I knew it was where the rally was taking place because a large group of women—all wearing frilly dresses, big hats, and purple, white, and green sashes—was gathered along one end. The middle of the park was marked out for some sort of field event, the way an American park might be marked out with a baseball diamond, (only this was more like a long stripe than a diamond) and no one was walking on that. There was a pavilion off to the side, but there were no women there, only men, and they seemed to be drinking bottles of beer, which struck me as odd so early in the day. The women kept to the far side of the field, busily setting up stalls and what looked like a stage.

When I caught up with Annie, she was covering a table with a white sheet, tying the corners to the table legs with twine to keep them from flapping in the

178

breeze.

"What is all this?" I asked, after she saw me and gave my hand a surreptitious squeeze.

"We need to provide refreshments," she said, "unless you think people will come from far and wide just to hear you talk."

I grimaced, making her laugh.

"Don't be like that. You only need to say what you said on Sunday. It will be a good thing for the women, and the men, to hear a man supporting our cause."

"A man, yes," I said, stepping back and indicating my lieutenant insignia. "But it might look as if I'm representing the military. Maybe I should be in civilian clothes. Your uncle Henry is going to be very upset if he hears about this."

She came to my side and took my arm. "Oh, but you look so handsome in your uniform. And don't worry about Henry, Maggie will calm him down, and your friend Brody will make sure he doesn't demote you."

She smiled, making dimples appear in her cheeks. I leaned in to kiss her, but she pulled away. When I frowned, she laughed again. "Oh, I do wish we were in your world. Is it truly possible to kiss someone right out in the open like this?"

I nodded. "You'd find it shocking."

"As well as delightful. But in my world, I'm afraid patience is still a virtue. Come, let's walk."

Still holding my arm, she pulled me past more tables, introducing me as we went along. There were so many women in the whirl of activity, that I didn't bother trying to remember names. Mostly the women, like Annie had been, were arranging tables around the outskirts of the group for refreshments, setting out cakes and cookies, and even some old-fashioned kettles containing hot water for tea. Other women—helped by a few men—were building makeshift booths out of rough boards, where they could hand out leaflets and suffragist ribbons and cajole people into signing petitions.

Then she brought me to Mrs. Thompson, who was supervising the construction of the stage. A dozen or so women had erected a small platform, but it looked about to fall over.

"Ah, there's your young man," she said as we drew near. "Just when we needed another strong pair of hands."

"We can't make him work," Annie said. "He's a guest speaker, and he'll ruin his uniform."

"Nonsense," Mrs. Thompson said. "We all need to pitch in."

"It's all right," I said, feeling slightly awkward, and seeing that the women really did need help. "I'll be careful."

Reluctantly, Annie gave in and left me with the construction crew. I took off my jacket, rolled up my sleeves, and tried to recall the little carpentry Dad had taught me.

They were working with an ancient version of two-by-fours, large panels of wood, square nails, and a lack of architectural know-how. There was plenty of wood available, and more coming in by horse cart, so building a larger, more robust, stage was possible, if I knew what I was doing. Fortunately, my presence attracted the attention of a few nearby men, who drafted in other men, and soon we had an actual crew with some useful skills. Taking the lead, they formulated a plan involving A-shaped braces, crossbeams, and a lot of nailing. By the time we were finished, and I was cooling down with a glass of lemon aide and slice of apple cake one of the women brought me, it was nearing three in the afternoon.

"It'll hold well enough," the man who had taken over as foreman told Mrs. Thompson.

She looked warily at the structure. "It's a bit ungainly. And awfully high."

"The better to see you," he said, smiling. When Mrs. Thompson didn't smile back, he continued. "We had no choice. With only one saw and no time to make cuts, we had to size the building to the wood, not the other way around. Don't worry, we put stairs in on one side."

Mrs. Thompson sighed. "Well, they wouldn't allow us to use the pavilion, so needs must. It is safe, isn't it?"

"Oh, yes," the man said. "The back has a solid wall. For stability. There wasn't any need to block off the front and sides."

In truth, there hadn't been any time, or wood, either.

Mrs. Thompson, still frowning, nodded. "Then I'm sure it will be fine. Thank you ever so much."

The man started to turn away, then stopped. "But I wouldn't have more than half a dozen folks up there at a time, mind."

Annie appeared as I was trying to make myself look only mildly dishevelled, and she and I helped fasten curtains around the stage to make it look more inviting. They weren't real curtains, just excess sheets they'd been using to cover tables, but with the stage being nearly twenty feet long and fifteen feet wide, some women who lived locally had to rush home to get more. I did one whole side while the women did the front but, when they saw how I'd done it, they made me take the sheets down so they could re-hang them, making ruffles and pleats as they tacked them up. I had to admit it looked better, but it took more time and even more sheets.

By now, the park was filling up, mostly with women wearing Suffragist colours. Near the pavilion, on the far side of the playing field—which I had been informed was something called a cricket pitch—more men were gathering. There were a few women with them, but none of them were wearing suffragist colours. Occasionally, one or two would turn our way and shout insults, calling us traitors and giving their opinion on what should be done to us, none of it pleasant.

"Pay them no mind," Annie told me when she saw me looking their way. "This happens at every rally. It's nothing unusual."

A row of chairs and a small lectern were put on the stage as the rally got underway. Those working took to their booths and tables, and those speaking climbed onto the stage. I followed Annie and took a seat at the end of the row. Annie wasn't going to speak, but I think Mrs. Thompson wanted her up there to make sure I didn't run away, or faint. It was a good move, as I felt like doing both.

Mrs. Thompson, standing behind the lectern, called for order and introduced the first speaker. The crowd gathered close to the stage and listened in silence as the woman spoke about the work they were doing and the contributions to society women had to offer, if only they got the vote.

"Woman and men," she said, "can work together, as equals, in a peaceful world."

"You're in the factories so you can sabotage them," one of the men yelled. "You want the Germans to win so you can push the men out."

Despite this not making much sense, his companions cheered him and booed the speaker. The woman continued, her voice never wavering. I had to admire her.

"Traitors," the men chanted. "Saboteurs." Then they started moving toward us, walking across the cricket pitch, gathering at the fringes of the rally. A few of the women on the stage looked at each other nervously. Annie gave my hand a squeeze. I looked at her. Her eyes were wide, her brow furrowed, and I began to think this was no longer, "Not unusual."

Chapter 26

Charlie

We decided to do nothing that night. Major Billings feared that Farber might be conspiring with others, and if so, we needed to find out who they were. So, we couldn't arrest Farber, not right then, at least. And we couldn't start looking into what damage Farber had done, either. If he saw the lab lights on in the middle of the night, he might worry that we were on to him and do a runner. So, we all went to bed for a few hours of much-needed sleep.

At first light, I met Major Billings and Captain Newell, as agreed, in the Major's office. Billings tried to appear in control by serenely smoking his pipe, but he looked as if he had slept in his clothes (as had I), and his face was grim and unshaven.

"We're in a bit of a bind here," he said, as I took a seat across from him and Captain Newell. "We don't dare tell the bases that the ammunition we supplied them yesterday has been sabotaged. It will stifle morale, and if the War Office gets wind of this, they'll shut us down."

"But they can't go up with those pans," I said. "The bullets won't work. They've got to be told."

Billings took a long puff on his pipe. "Those boys don't need bad news. They need good bullets."

"So, what are we going to do?"

"Get them some good ammunition as soon as possible."

I shook my head. "But Farber contaminated the last of the mixture. There's none of the chemicals we need left. We'll have to order more, and that will take—"

Captain Newell stopped me with a smile and a raised hand. "There's always a drop or two left in the bottle," he said.

"You mean …"

Billings nodded. "Captain Jeffreys is in the lab right now, scraping together what he can. He says he thinks he can scavenge enough to make a small batch. Enough for four, maybe five hundred rounds."

"That many?"

"The chemicals we had to order are the lynchpin," Billings said. "The other chemicals we have in abundance. And we only need a small amount of the critical ingredients."

"We could make enough to fill a dozen 47-round pans," Newell added. "Not enough to go around, but we could supply a single base."

Billings puffed his pipe again. "Sutton's Farm, at Hornchurch, would be my preference. They have the best pilots."

For the first time, I felt a smattering of hope. But...

"What about Farber? How do we keep him from finding out what we're doing?"

"We struck lucky there, son," Billings said. "Captain Farber will not be on the base today. He'd arranged for a pass some time ago."

"That's convenient," I said, "but also suspicious."

Billings rubbed the stubble on his chin. "Agreed.

185

But at least it takes care of one of our problems. The other—"

He was cut short by a rap on the door. Captain Newell opened it and ushered in Sergeant Dobson, who stood to attention in the centre of the room.

"At ease, sergeant," Billings said. "Let's hear it."

"Captain Farber is currently having his breakfast. Sergeant Orr is keeping him under observation. Before he entered the officer's mess, he requested a car from the Motor Pool."

Billings nodded. "See that he gets one. And prepare a vehicle for yourselves. You, Sergeant Orr and Captain Wyman will follow him when he leaves the base."

"Yes, sir."

"Discreetly," added Newell.

Dobson saluted and left.

"Shouldn't I stay here?" I asked as soon as I heard the door close. "If I help with the bullets, we can finish them in half the time." I was disappointed, not so much because I wanted to make bullets, but with nothing much to do until Captain Jeffreys finished the formula, I was hoping I could go back to bed for a few hours.

Billings shook his head. "No attack is going to come during the day. As long as we have the ammunition ready for Lieutenant Brody by this evening, he can get the pans to Sutton's Farm before the pilots take off for their patrols. Captain Jeffreys will have the formula mixed and ready by noon and he and Captain Newell will assemble the ammunition while you are solving the other problem: finding out what Farber is up to."

"But Sergeant Orr and Sergeant Dobson seem to

have that under control," I said, still hoping for some time in bed.

Billings leaned forward and lowered his voice. "They do, but you are better suited to follow Captain Farber than either of them."

"What do you mean, better suited?"

Captain Newell raised his eyebrows. "You're a spy, aren't you?" It wasn't a question; it was a statement.

I looked from Newell to Billings and said nothing.

Billings inclined his head toward the door. "So, go spy."

◆

Outside, it was getting lighter, though the sun was not yet up. Dobson was walking in the opposite direction from the mess halls and barracks, heading, I supposed, to the Motor Pool. In the other direction, in front of the officers' mess, Sergeant Orr was lingering, pretending to inspect the grounds while he waited for Farber to finish his breakfast.

I turned and followed Dobson.

The Motor Pool looked more like a warehouse than a garage. The front of the building was taken up with two huge swinging doors, and next to them was a normal-sized door that Dobson entered.

"Looks like we'll be working together," I said, as I stepped inside after him.

"Yes, sir," he said, saluting.

I returned his salute, already tired of the traditions and expectations of the officer class. "So, what are we to do?"

He shrugged. "Get an automobile ready, sir."

I looked at the vehicles lined up in the dim light:

187

two Model-A cars and three old-fashioned trucks with wide, open beds, useful for carrying men as well as equipment. It looked like a museum, until Dobson turned on the lights. Then the cars no longer looked like antiques: the paint was new, and the black walls of the tires shone.

"We're a small base, sir," Dobson said, as I continued to stare at them. "Only three autos and five trucks."

I mentally counted two cars and three trucks.

"Some are out, at present, sir," Dobson said.

I nodded. "I see. And stop calling me Sir."

"Yes, sir," he said. "I mean, yes."

Being an officer did have its advantages, though, because I wasn't expected to work. This was a good thing because I had no idea what getting a car like that ready involved. So, I stood back and watched as Dobson filled the tank, using a funnel and a can of gas, and turning a crank to start the engine. Only then did he ask for my help, and it was a little embarrassing needing to have him show me what levers to push and knobs to pull and pedals to step on to get the engine revved up while, at the same time, not running Dobson over.

When Orr arrived, he and Dobson opened the big doors and drove the car outside leaving it to idle noisily on the forecourt as they cleaned the windows and polished the fenders. But Farber was not yet ready to leave, it seemed. I saw him in the distance, at the front gate, talking with Corporal Blake. Then I saw Mitch, who was walking toward them from the direction of the airplane hangar. He stopped to talk with Blake and Farber, though I suspected he was simply showing his pass. Blake let him out and, once

Mitch was gone, he and Farber talked a little more.

On his way to the Motor Pool, Farber detoured into the officer's quarters and emerged carrying a small suitcase. I slipped inside the Motor Pool to keep out of sight as it might make him suspicious to see the three of us there waiting for him. Dobson had turned off the light, so I stood in the shadows and watched as Farber tossed the leather case into the rear of the automobile—nothing explosive, then—and drove away.

As soon as the car passed through the gate, Orr and Dobson ran to one of the trucks. Orr jumped into the driver's seat while Dobson worked a crank on the front of the truck to make it start.

"Come on," he said, climbing up beside Orr.

I squeezed in and Orr drove onto the forecourt and headed toward the gate.

"Open up, Corporal," Orr said as he rolled the truck to a stop next to Blake.

"Pass?"

Orr leaned out the window. "We're under orders. Major Billings. He wants us to go into town."

"You can't leave without a pass," Blake said. "Regulations."

Orr sighed and Dobson leaned forward, no doubt getting ready to give Blake an ear full, but I knew it wouldn't do any good; Blake was right, we needed a pass.

"Go to the Major and get one," I said to Dobson, opening the door and stepping out.

That was another advantage of being an officer. Dobson, without a word, jumped out of the truck and ran. He was back in less than five minutes, barely winded.

"Here, sir," he said, handing me a scrap of paper. "I mean, here."

I took the paper and handed it to Blake. All it said was, "Open the gate!" But it was signed by Major Billings and that was enough. I got back in the truck and Blake unlatched the gate. Orr pulled forward, then stopped.

"That man's an officer, corporal," he said. "You're expected to salute."

Blake scowled but snapped his hand up to his forehead. I saluted in return, and we sped away.

"He's keen on regulations," Orr observed as we gained speed, "but only those that suit him."

After that, we concentrated on following Farber. He had quite a head start, but the morning was still, and the road was dusty, so he left a trail and, of course, there was nowhere else to go. We bounced along with Orr staring into the dust cloud, traveling at a speed I didn't think the truck was capable of.

"Who's that?" Orr asked.

Both Dobson and I peered ahead.

"That's my brother," I said, ducking behind the dashboard.

"But—"

"But nothing. Just keep driving. Don't even look at him. If he sees me, we'll have to stop and offer him a ride."

"You can ignore your brother," Orr said, "but we can't ignore an officer. What's he going to think?"

"I don't care what he thinks, sergeant," I said, "I only care about catching up with Farber."

"Yes, sir."

My head thumped against the dashboard as I struggled to stay low.

"And please stop calling me 'Sir.'"

"Yes … Captain."

Another bump. Then another.

"Ah, you can sit up now, Captain," Dobson said, a slight smirk on his face. "We left your brother behind some time ago."

We passed several roads that Farber could have turned down, but the dust trail told us we were on the right track and, incredibly, when we got close to town, we were slowed down by traffic, and there, in front of us, was Farber. He turned north and, not wanting to be obvious, we let a few cars go ahead of us before following.

If you think being a spy is a cool job, think again. I can't remember when I spent such a boring day. We followed him from Earlswood to Redhill, where he parked. So, we had to find a place to park the truck and catch up with Farber on foot. Then we spent hours sneaking around, watching him walk from the middle of town to the gasworks on the south edge of town, to the sports ground on the north end of town—where people were gathering for the rally and where we had to keep a double look-out to make sure Mitch didn't spot us and give us away—and back again.

After that, Farber bought a paper, had coffee, read, wandered into a few shops, ate lunch in a restaurant, and spent some time in the local library, all the while keeping his leather case close to hand. The only good thing about it was we each had time to sneak off to get something to eat and drink while the other two kept their eyes on Farber. At around one o'clock, after looking at his pocket watch for the hundredth time, he went to a small hotel just off the main street, a place Dobson called a Boarding House, and rented a room.

That gave us our first real problem. If he was meeting someone, we needed to follow him, but that wasn't going to be as easy as watching him eat lunch through a restaurant window. Standing a discreet distance from the hotel, we debated what to do about it.

"I think we should just go in and tell the landlord who we are and what we're doing," Orr said. "He'll tell us what room Farber is in, and who is with him."

"If he believes us," Dobson said. "Our story is proper flimsy."

"But we've got a Captain with us."

Dobson looked at me. "As I said, a flimsy story. And Captain Farber is the same rank, and he can be quite convincing."

"We have to do something," Orr said. "He could be in there, making plans with some Kraut spy right now."

I half listened to them while watching people pass on the street; a man entered, then another, and another, and any of them might be the person Farber was waiting for. Or, the person might be inside already, waiting for Farber, assuming, of course, there was another person. For all we knew, Farber was acting alone. Then a man on the opposite sidewalk stopped. He was tall and skinny and carrying a large suitcase. He looked left, then right, then crossed the road and climbed the steps to the hotel.

"And what if they call the police on us—"

I stopped Dobson with a tap on the shoulder.

"I know who Farber is meeting," I said, pointing.

Both Orr and Dobson turned to see the man step

through the door. It was the man with the petitions and the big voice, the man me and Mitch had seen on our first day in the Carfax, the man who had attacked us during the riot.

I ran to the boarding house and peeked through the door in time to see the man still talking to the landlord, who wasn't a landlord, but a landlady. The reception room was small and dark and spare, with only an ornate table serving as a desk, where a leather-bound book lay open, although the landlady—a formidable woman wearing a tent-like dress cinched at the waist—was leaning over the pages, hiding whatever was written on the pages from view.

"My associate would have left instructions," the man was saying.

The landlady looked up at him with dark, angry eyes.

"Aye, he did but that no means I'd agreed to them. I run an orderly house. No women friends in the rooms, and certainly no man friends."

The skinny man stood straight, clutching his suitcase. "I take exception to what you are insinuating, madam. I am here on Government business."

"And I'm the Queen of Sheba. You want to go up, you rent a room like anybody else."

The man nodded. "I see." He reached in his pocket with his free hand and came out with some bills. Only then did the landlady straighten up. She stuffed the bills into her bra, opened a drawer on the back of the table, and pulled out a key while the man studied the register.

The man looked down at her. "I don't need a key," he said, heading for the stairs.

"I hear anything," the landlady said, "anything at all, I'll have the coppers on you."

The man ignored her. She dropped the key into the drawer and turned away, toward a door in the back of the room as Dobson and Orr came up behind me. I waved at them to keep back but she must have seen the movement because, just before she closed the door, she spotted me.

"What do you want, sonny?"

I stepped into the reception area, trying to look confident. "A room."

"I don't like soldiers in my house," she said. "Soldiers are trouble."

I went up to the table to look at the register, but she got there first and leaned forward to cover it.

"No girls, no booze," the landlady said, "and I lock the door at 10 o'clock. You're not in, you sleep on the street."

"Yes, Ma'am," I said.

"Now show me your money."

I pulled out the bills Maggie had given me, hoping they would be enough. The landlady looked at me suspiciously, then took a few and pushed the rest back toward me.

"American?"

"Canadian," I said, pocketing the bills.

"They don't teach you to count?"

I didn't answer. She rummaged in the drawer, came up with a key and handed it to me.

"Room eight. Sign here."

As I did, I scanned the names. Three up from mine was the name, "Captain Featherstone," with "Room 4" next to it. I took the key and went up the stairs.

My room was on the top floor, but I wasn't going there. I went down the hallway on the second floor and found room four. After checking that no one was in the hallway, I knelt to look through the keyhole. In my world, looking through a keyhole is impossible, but back then, key holes were so enormous you could easily see through them. I didn't do it for long, though, because someone might come by at any minute. So, I only stayed their long enough to see the skinny man open his suitcase and take out a metal box.

"This is the device," he said. "Made to your specifications."

"And I have the explosives," Farber said.

I didn't wait to hear any more. I walked quietly away, then rushed down the stairs and headed for the door. Before I got there, however, the landlady burst out of the back room and screeched at me. "Where do you think you're going?"

"Out," I said.

"The key."

"Pardon?"

"Leave the key."

I put it on the table. She snatched it up and dropped it in the drawer.

"Remember," she said, heading back into the room, "no visitors, and the doors are locked at ten sharp."

"Yes, Ma'am."

As soon as she was gone, I walked to the door and motioned Dobson and Orr to come with me, quietly. We sneaked up the stairs and tiptoed to room four.

"What do we do now?" Dobson whispered. "We're sitting ducks out here."

"We need to find out what they're doing," I whispered back.

"How?" Orr asked.

"We could get into the room next door," Dobson said. "Listen through the wall."

"How?" Orr asked again. "We don't have a key."

Dobson looked at me. "Maybe you could sneak downstairs and pretend you're coming back. That way you could get your key."

I shook my head. "What good would that do?"

"It might fit the lock on room three."

"That's ridiculous," Orr said. "We should just try to pick it."

"Good idea," Dobson said. "Do you have a hairpin on you?"

Orr glared at him and was about to reply when I tried the door to room three and it opened.

The room was empty, so we ducked inside and closed the door. Someone had obviously rented the room because there was a small suitcase next to the bureau, but they had apparently left without locking the door. It seemed a strange thing to do but I didn't waste time wondering about it. I just put my ear to the wall and listened.

It was difficult to hear, so I held my breath, closed my eyes, and concentrated.

"… and this will go off at seven?" Farber's voice.

"On the dot."

"… take it with me … shift change … night manager install it."

"He's … blow himself up?"

Farber laughed; that came through clear enough. "… a bit dull … spun him a yarn … helping with the war effort."

"… wait until seven?"

"… half an hour before … get the excitement started …"

It was confusing, and then I began to wonder why someone would leave a door unlocked, and it hit me that it might be someone who knew they had to leave the key at the desk when they left and who then wanted to sneak back in with a guest.

"We have to go," I said. "Now."

But just then the door opened and a young woman, with hair that was a bit too blonde, wearing make-up that was a bit too thick, and clothes that were a bit too tight, entered, followed by a man in a grey suit. They both looked at us with startled expressions. Then the woman started yelling.

"What are you trying to pull," she said, but not to us. She was yelling at the guy in the suit. "I'm not that sort of girl. This isn't what we agreed. I don't know what you're thinking, but this is going to cost you more …"

We tried to shush her, but she ignored us. Then we heard feet pounding up the stairs and the landlady stepped into the threshold. The woman finally went quiet as we all stared in shock. The landlady glared at us, her fists on her ample hips. Then, without a word, she backed into the hallway and slammed the door. The click of a key sounded in the silence, and I realized we had just been locked in.

The man in the suit looked at the floor, shaking his head, his shoulders slumped, while the woman pounded on the door, shouting that she wasn't that sort of girl. We tried to get her to stop, but she just kept on until, a few minutes later, the door opened, and four policemen entered.

Chapter 27

Mitch

By the time the third speaker was halfway through her talk, the mob—for that's what it had turned into—was making so much noise only those nearest the stage could hear her. I was to speak next, and I wasn't sure how that was going to go. Firstly, I had no idea what to say, and secondly, would anyone hear me, and finally, what would the men think of someone like me speaking up for women. It might get even uglier.

As it was, more men were arriving, and bulking out the number of protesters on the fringes. Then they began pushing some of the women around. I noticed a few policemen on the periphery of the crowd, but they didn't seem interested in trying to keep order. Soon, the shoving became more violent. A woman, held by two burly men, screamed. The few who came to her aid—both men and women—got into fistfights with other members of the mob.

Then they started overturning tables. Cups, saucers, and teapots flew through the air. A Votes For Women banner was torn down. More fights broke out, and the mob surged into the crowd. The few policemen finally rushed into the fray, but instead of going after the mob, they went after the women, swinging their batons.

The women surrounding the stage pressed into a tight circle, fighting with placards, umbrellas, and fists, but they were no match for the mob. The men waded into them, punching, kicking, and moving like a slow, unstoppable wave, toward the stage. Annie and the others stared at the spectacle, their faces white.

Then I looked into the crowd, at the police advancing on the women, and the men advancing on the stage. As the mob came closer, I saw a tall, skinny man leading the main charge. My jaw dropped and my grip on Annie's hand tightened. It was the man with the big voice, and he was looking up at me.

Chapter 28

Charlie

They locked us all in the same cell, because it was the only one they had. The man in the suit went completely silent and sat on the hard bench with his head in his hands. The woman seemed to be a friend of the officers. They called her by name and joked with her as she sat on the bench, with her arms folded and a bored expression on her face.

The police didn't want to hear anything from us. We tried to tell them that we were on a mission, but they threatened to use their billy-clubs on us if we didn't stop talking, so we did. Then they yelled at us for making a mess of their town and accused us of all sorts of bad behaviour. I guess the soldiers stationed in the nearby bases hadn't made a good impression on the local people, which was bad for us because the police weren't interested in anything we had to say; they were only interested in making us uncomfortable.

And we were. Uncomfortable, that is. I tried to sleep but the bench was hard and narrow, and the police were making too much noise. The station wasn't large, just a big room with a hallway at one end that led, I supposed, to more rooms, but all the action seemed to take place where we were. Wooden file cabinets, with drawers half-open and papers spilling out, lined the back wall. In front of them was a large and equally cluttered desk where the chief sat, and in front of the desk was an open area where several junior officers mingled. Tucked into the corner furthest from the door was an iron cage with the five of us crammed inside it.

About an hour after we were brought in, a middle-aged woman wearing too much make-up and too tight clothes arrived. She chatted with the policemen, paid a fine and they released the young woman into her care. Sometime later a very angry woman barged into the station. She ignored the police and shouted at the man, who cowered in the corner. The police then released him, though I suspect he would have rather stayed in the cell. They left together, with the woman still yelling, and the man with his head hanging low.

"A business meeting," she said. "Out of town, you said. Not back until late, you said. Is that where you've been spending all your so-called business meetings? I've a mind to call your boss, and your mother …"

You could still hear her even when they were half a block away.

We tried to talk to the police again, but they were tired of shouting at us and simply ignored us, so we could do nothing but sit on the bench and wait. I looked around the office. On the wall was a large clock with a swinging pendulum. It read two-thirty-seven.

◆

Two and a half hours later, we were still there, still sitting on the bench, still pleading with any policeman within range to let us out, and still being ignored.

At around five o'clock, the chief—a stout man with a walrus moustache and a uniform decked out in gold buttons—gathered all available officers into the station. And it was all available. Redhill was a good-sized town by 1916 standards, but they couldn't have that many police on shift; it had to be the entire force, and perhaps others from neighbouring towns. They crowded into the office and lined up at attention: older men no longer eligible for military service, younger men not ready for service, and a scattering of soldier-aged men who must have had a good reason to be in the police force instead of at the front fighting. The chief, his gold buttons straining against his puffed-out chest, strutted in front of them.

"You have an important mission tonight, men," he told them. "Those women, in our park, at the edge of our town, those so-called suffragettes, want more than the vote."

He stopped and looked from man to man. "They are subversives, agitators, traitors, looking to take our jobs and run our country. And they are not shy about using violence to achieve their ends."

Despite the men being at attention, a murmur of assent rumbled through the room.

"We have it on good authority," he continued, "that these suffragette saboteurs are planning something. Something big. An act of treachery aimed at crippling the war effort. And it is our job to stop them."

More murmurs. The chief smiled.

Having seen the skinny man from the Carfax plotting with Farber, I had a feeling I knew where the rumours were coming from, but the police didn't question the source or speculate on its truthfulness, they openly grumbled about "uppity women" and what they were going to do to them.

"When the time comes," the chief continued, "I expect you all to do your duty. You are to arrest and detain as many of the agitators as you can. And you are to place expediency above decorum. These are dangerous people, saboteurs, traitors; they have forfeited their right to gentle handling."

The policemen lost all sense of decorum. Without being dismissed, they turned to one another, smiling and talking, testing bully clubs, and checking handcuffs. I began to worry about Mitch and Annie, as well as the others at the rally. The civilian men already hated them, and now the police were against them. They could be in big trouble. I hoped that at least some of the officers might take the women's side, but then I noticed something distressing.

"The police," I said to Dobson. "They're all men. Where are the women officers?"

Dobson looked at me and rolled his eyes. "Women officers? You're joking, right?"

Then the door opened, and another officer entered, an old man wearing an ill-fitting uniform and a pair of thick glasses. Orr speculated that it might be the night-shift captain, who had probably been pulled out of retirement because so many men were off fighting the war. It seemed they were going to leave him in charge while they—with the chief leading the way—marched to the Suffragette rally to deal with the subversives.

That worried me even more, but then the chief came over to the cell, and finally turned his attention to us.

"Lucky for you," he said, "we need all the room available for those seditious women. So, I'm going to call your commanding officer and tell him to come fetch you so he can put you in a military prison. Now, tell me how to contact your base."

After Dobson told him he went to his desk, picked up a type of telephone I had once seen in a museum, clicked the lever a few times, and shouted numbers. Then he waited.

"This is Chief Thurgood of Redhill constabulary," he said, using his best authoritarian voice. "I have three of your men in my jail, arrested for participating in indecent acts in a local hotel. Our good town does not abide this sort of depravity— What? Well, I never asked."

Put off his stride, but still feeling righteous, he held the phone away from his mouth and looked our way.

"Names!"

"Captain Wyman," I said, "and Sergeants Dobson and Orr."

The chief only got my name out before he stopped, sputtered a few times, and turned the colour of newly ripened strawberries.

"But I couldn't know. No, we ... I ... yes ... yes, sir."

Then he turned away from the phone and shouted at an officer. "Release those men at once."

I tried to keep from grinning as I stepped out of the cell, but neither Dobson nor Orr made any such attempt.

"He wants to talk to you," the chief said, thrusting the phone at me.

"Report," Billings said, as soon as I got the phone

204

to my ear.

I turned away, conscious that Chief Thurgood was hovering close. "We followed the, uh, target. He met with another individual, known to me—"

"To you?"

"Yes. A subversive, and a saboteur." I glanced toward the chief and narrowed my eyes. He took the hint and backed away, out of earshot. "He and Farber constructed a bomb. Farber is going to place it."

"Where?"

"I don't know. We were interrupted before I could gather that intelligence. All I know is, wherever the bomb is, it will go off at seven this evening—"

"Well, do something, son."

"I will," I said. "But there's more. The saboteur is going to stir up trouble at the rally. The rally where your niece is. And the police have been instructed to harass the women and arrest them."

Billings sputtered. "What? The police? You sure?"

I lowered my voice to make sure no one heard. "Positive. The chief, he was just briefing his men about using billy-clubs and handcuffs on the women. Annie is in danger, sir."

"You tell that traitorous … never mind. I'll tell him myself. But you stay there until I arrive to make sure no one leaves."

"Yes, sir."

I handed the phone back to the chief, who sputtered and went red again, and said, "Yessir," and "Nosir," a couple of times before hanging up.

Every officer in the room watched as the chief put the phone back on his desk, pulled his revolver out of its holster and offered it to me.

"What's this for?" I asked.

He glanced at the officers, then down at the floor. "You're to use it to shoot anyone who tries to leave."

I waved the gun away and stepped back. "That's okay. But no one better leave until Major Billings arrives, or you'll have him to answer to."

Twenty minutes later, I heard the rattle of a truck and the screech of brakes, and a few seconds later Billings burst through the door. He didn't look at anyone, he just marched to the desk, pushed Chief Thurgood aside and faced the startled officers, as a dozen soldiers armed with rifles crammed into the crowded room.

"Now listen here," he bellowed. "We are going to the rally. There is a subversive element there, and it is not the women. You will keep order, assist us in apprehending the guilty parties, and protect the women. After this operation is over, I intend to interview every one of those women, and if any of them tells me a policeman so much as laid a finger on them, I will find that officer and make sure he is on the next boat to France. Is that clear?"

The officers, their faces pale, looked to their chief, who continued to gaze at the floor. A wave of "Yes sirs" rolled through the room.

"There are two transport trucks outside," Billings continued. "You will ride in them to the rally, where every soldier, and every officer, will perform his duty faithfully. Now is that—"

His words were cut short as someone crashed through the door, shouting that a riot had broken out at the rally.

I looked at the clock. It was six-thirty-two.

Chapter 29

Mitch

Brawling men and women surrounded us, screaming, shouting, punching, bleeding. Wounded women clambered onto the stage, with men behind them. The half-dozen women lined up beside us grabbed their chairs and began bashing at the men with them. Annie ran to the edge of the stage to help pull a woman out of the grip of a policeman, while two other women beat him with signs. As she bent down to grab the woman's arms, the skinny man with the big voice reached up for her.

"Annie, no," I said. "Get back."

"What do you expect us to do?" she asked, still attempting to pry the woman out of the policeman's grasp. "Give up?"

I rushed up behind her. "You don't understand. That man—"

And then she was gone.

I looked over the edge. Even in the shifting sea of people, they would have been easy to spot, but they had disappeared. With rising panic, I looked left, and right, and then down. The curtain below was ripped, exposing the underside of the stage. I jumped down, pushed the policeman aside, and slipped inside.

It was dim, but light enough to see. In the oasis of calm, the riot faded to a roar, as if a giant beast stood just outside, bellowing in frustration and batting at the structure with a massive paw. Against the back wall, the man held a knife against Annie's throat.

"Don't hurt her," I said.

"I knew you'd come for her. You seem the type. Now stay where you are if you don't want to see your sweetheart with her throat slit."

I stopped. We stared at each other for a few moments, aware that—with the crowd crushing tighter against the stage—the stand-off could not go on for long.

"Come forward," he said. "Slowly."

I stepped toward them, keeping an eye on the knife.

"Up against that post. And hold your hands out behind you."

Still holding the knife against Annie's throat, he dragged her forward and threw her down at my feet.

"Your turn now," he said, switching the knife to me, pressing the tip painfully into the soft flesh beneath my jaw. "If you don't want to see your young man's blood ruin his fine uniform, tie his hands."

Annie used her suffragette sash to bind my wrists, making it good and loose. But before I could work free, the man knocked Annie to the ground, pulled the knots painfully tight and grabbed her again as she tried to get up. With quick, smooth movements, he pinned her arms behind her back, picked up a piece of twine from the ground and bound her so tightly she moaned in pain. But still, she kept fighting.

"Keep it up," he told her, "and I'll pluck one of his eyes out. After I force you to choose which one."

She calmed down and allowed him to sit her down against the rear wall. Above us, thuds, screams, and

208

tramping feet echoed as more and more people climbed onto the stage, but down in the dim light, there was only us, and an eerie calm, punctuated by the creaking of the uprights.

At the sound of a sharp crack, the man looked up and sighed.

"Pity," he said. "I was hoping to have a bit of fun with the girl before I killed you. But as we're short on time, I'll just slit your throats and be done with it."

I felt faint and took a slow breath to clear my head.

"This is a little extreme for ruining your petition."

The man laughed. "My petition? What you interfered with was our plan to get Britain out of the war. Once that happens there will be nothing to stop our victory."

"Traitor," Annie said.

"Patriot," the man said. "I, and my comrades, are loyal to the Kaiser, and when the Zeppelins attack and the population realizes there is no defence against them, they will demand your government's capitulation."

"Not if we shoot them down," Annie said. "We've got new weapons. You can't win."

The man looked down at her. "Let's see if you can talk as bravely with an extra smile."

"She's right," I said, hoping to distract him. "The pilots, we made new ammunition for them. Bullets that can take down a Zeppelin."

Above, the tramping grew louder. The upright behind me bowed and I heard an ominous crack.

"You think you've got it all figured out," he said, coming toward me. "Your puny little outfit can't best a German airship." He held the knife in front of my face, the blade touching the tip of my nose. "I think, before you die, I'll tell you what's true, so you can go to your maker knowing that you failed." He pulled a watch from his pocket and looked at it. "In ten minutes, half this town is going to go up in flames, and every available man within a ten-mile radius is going to be busy fighting the fire. There will be no one to man the searchlights as the biggest Zeppelin raid in history flies to your capital undetected."

"But, the bullets …"

"Useless. We've neutralized them all. Your efforts have been doomed from the start. Now, I think it's time to say good-bye."

I felt hollow and cold. Could it be true? If so, I had to warn them. But I couldn't see that happening. My shoulders slumped; my head drooped.

"Ah, now you understand. But I think I'll do the girl first, just to complete your humiliation."

He turned toward Annie. Panic overwhelmed me. Then I heard another creak and realized we did have a chance. A slim one, but I had to try.

I lunged forward. The upright bent, my wrists throbbed, but nothing happened. The man looked at me and laughed. I lunged again. This time, the upright gave way, breaking in two just above my head. I stumbled forward, past the man, and dove on top of Annie as more uprights snapped like rifle fire and the stage floor collapsed in a cascade of tangled wood and screaming women.

Chapter 30

Charlie

When Major Billings said he had two trucks, he meant he had one and we had the other. But ours was some distance away, so while he ordered soldiers and policemen onto his truck and drove away, we led a second group on a quick march through the streets to where Orr had parked ours. The men jumped in back. Dobson and I squeezed into the cab with Orr.

We were pointing the wrong way on a narrow side street, so Orr had to circle the block to get back to the main road, which was packed with cars, horse carriages, and people. Orr beeped the horn and bulled his way onto the road. I willed the truck forward, aware that time was against us. Farber had planted a bomb, but where? Was it at the rally? If so, we'd never get there in time, and if we did, what good could we do? The bomb could be anywhere.

"Can't you go any faster," I said.

"I'm doing my best. sir," Orr said, startling two horses as he roared between a carriage and an oncoming car.

"It's only this crowded because of shift change," Dobson said. "Once we get further from the gasworks, it should thin out."

"What did you say?"

"That it should thin out."

"No," I said. "Before that. About the gasworks."

Dobson looked at me as if he thought I was slow. "The shift changed a while ago. That's why the road is so—"

I grabbed him by his arm, opened the door and jumped out, dragging the startled sergeant with me.

"Orr, get to the rally," I shouted, slamming the door. "Dobson, with me. I know where the bomb is."

I ran back the way we had come, with Dobson loping beside me.

"What's going on?"

"The shift change," I said. "I overheard Farber say something about it, and the night manager. We need to get to the gasworks. That's where Farber took the bomb."

"Are you sure?"

"As I can be. Now where is the gasworks. Take me to it."

"Follow me, sir."

Dobson picked up the pace and I struggled to keep up. We raced down the street, dodging carts, horses, and trucks, and soon arrived at a jumbled collection of buildings connected by massive pipes and power lines, and lit by harsh electric lights. It was a huge, confusing mass of brick and iron, with men hurrying from one building to another. We were about to collar one and ask where to find the main office when a greasy-haired young man darted out of a wooden hut at the edge of the compound.

"You there! Where do you think you're going?" He stopped in front of us, blocking our path, wheezing from the short run. "Unauthorized persons are not allowed in this area."

"And who are you?" I asked, trying to sound

authoritative. He eyed us suspiciously, then said, "I'm the shift manager."

This fit with the little I had heard Farber say.

"You were visited earlier," I said, hoping my hunch was right. "An officer, like me. He gave you something. A package, in a suitcase. Where is it?"

He went silent. I could tell he was thinking hard. Then he looked me in the eye and puffed out his chest. "That's a matter of national security. I am not allowed to tell you."

"This is a matter of national security," I said. "That man was a German spy, and that package was a bomb."

"He warned me someone like you might come," he said, shaking his head. "You are the spies. He's a patriot, and I'm a patriot. I am going to report this to the police and have you—"

Dobson was on him before I could even think to move, grabbing him by the shirt and pulling him up to his face.

"You've been duped, you dullard. This place is about to blow sky high, and if you don't help us find that bomb, I promise you, I'll make sure you survive the blast, so I can get you in front of a firing squad."

Then the man started blubbering and I felt a little sorry for him, seeing as how he was probably just a guy who, disappointed about not being able to join the army, jumped at a chance to do something he thought was important for the war effort. But there wasn't time for a soft approach, so I told him to stop crying and start talking.

"The officer, the one that came," he said between sobs, "he was here last week. He told me he was from a secret army unit, and that I had been selected to help with a top-secret mission. He had intelligence that enemy agents were going to target the gasworks. He needed me to place a device the army had developed, one that could detect the presence of bombs. I was to tell no one. It was top secret. He came back today and gave me the device. And I put it … I put it in a place where I thought a bomb would do the most damage. So, the device could detect any bombs, like he said."

"How much stupid can fit into one person," Dobson said, shaking the sobbing man to punctuate each word.

"Take us," I said. "Now."

Still sniffling, the man headed into the maze of buildings. Dobson pushed him between the shoulder-blades. "Faster. And don't even think about trying to run. I'll be on you before you take five steps, and you won't be happy when I catch you."

The man nodded and stepped up the pace. We trotted behind—Dobson keeping an eye on him, and me shouting to anyone I saw that they needed to evacuate the premises, pronto. Soon, men were scurrying everywhere, calling to one another, clearing all the buildings. The exodus grew from a trickle to a wave, as every man in the complex stampeded our way. We pushed through, and soon the wave subsided, leaving only a few stragglers, their footfalls echoing in the sudden silence as they ran for their lives.

The man led us deeper into the gasworks, steering us into a warehouse-sized building filled with pipes and valves and dials. Stepping over several thin pipes running parallel to the floor, he pointed at a large pipe behind them, about two feet in diameter and three feet off the concrete floor.

"It's there," he said.

"Where?"

"Behind."

I looked. Lashed to the pipe with a metal band was the suitcase.

"Get it off," I said.

He shook his head. "I can't. It's bolted on."

"Then unbolt it," Dobson said.

"It's … I'd need tools."

"Find some," I said.

The man scurried off. I looked around. There was a metal bar leaning against the far wall. I ran and got it.

"Help me," I said, forcing the end of the bar between the metal strip and the pipe.

Me and Dobson pulled. The metal band wasn't thick; it began to bend. I shoved the bar further beneath it. We pulled again, hard, and the bolts gave way with a pop, sending us, and the suitcase, to the floor. I grabbed it, slid it into the corridor and scrambled after it.

A deep crease ran across the top from where the metal strip had dug in, but it was otherwise undamaged. It was also locked. I was about to retrieve the metal bar to see if I could bash it open, but then the man returned, lugging a battered toolbox.

"That's a miracle," Dobson said under his breath as the man approached, "I'd have bet my life we'd never see him again."

"Hammer," I said, looking down at the suitcase and holding out my hand. After a brief clanking of metal, he gave me one. I smashed the lock and flipped the suitcase open.

Inside was a metal box. I lifted it out, kicked the suitcase away and set the box on the floor. It was newly made, the edges sharp, the joints smooth and the top bolted tight with screws that reflected the light. Attached to one end was a pocket watch. Attached to the watch were two wires, a red one and a green one, looping into the box through small holes.

"What is that?" the man asked.

"The bomb," I said. "And we need to find a way to defuse it before seven o'clock."

Dobson looked at the watch. "Three minutes, sir."

"Then we need to hurry." I held out my hand. "Screwdriver."

Nothing. I looked up. The man was gone.

"That's more like it," Dobson said. Then he pointed at the wires. "It looks to me like these are the triggers. If we pull them out, that should do the trick."

He reached down and grabbed the green wire.

Chapter 31

Mitch

Shouts of anger turned to screams of panic as the stage crumpled to the ground and the back wall pitched forward, trapping us in a tiny lean-to.

"I can't breathe," Annie said.

I was lying on top of her, and the wall was lying on top of me, pinning us painfully together. I tried to wiggle off her, but with our hands still tied, it was hard to move. I managed to squirm to one side as she shuffled the other way, and then I flopped, face down, next to her. The wall sank lower but didn't crush us.

"Better," Annie said, drawing a breath.

Around us the screaming continued. Footsteps thumped in every direction, tramping on the ground, thudding on the boards above us. I heard more cracking sounds, and for a moment thought some of the stage must still be falling, but it wasn't uprights splintering, it was real rifle fire.

A new level of shouting rose above the din. Not the angry shouts of protesters, these were commands, military commands.

"On their flank, men," the voice roared. More rifle fire, and the trill of police whistles. "Round up the lot of them. If a man so much as moves, shoot him on the spot. But take care with the women. And find my

217

niece."

"That's Uncle Henry," Annie said, kicking at the wall. "Here! We're here."

I helped as much as I could, hammering with my heels and raising my face from the grass to shout. Then the boards began to shift. Hands reached under, groping, grabbing my arms, pulling me, and Annie, from beneath the ruined stage. Soldiers and dishevelled women in suffragist colours surrounded us. Then Major Billings pushed through and knelt next to Annie.

"What happened?" he asked, untying her hands. "What did he do?"

One of the soldiers freed me and helped me to my feet. The major, still clutching Annie, glared up at me. "I'll have you court marshalled. And shot."

Annie pushed him away, jumped up and gripped me in a fierce hug. "You'll do no such thing." Then she kissed me, full on the lips, in front of everyone. A collective gasp rose from the crowd. Annie turned to face her uncle. "He saved my life. The other man was going to kill me. He had a knife."

"Other man?" Billings asked. "What other man?"

"He'd be under there, sir," I said, pointing to the wreckage.

Soldiers flung boards and broken uprights aside until they found him and dragged him into the twilight. He was bleeding from half a dozen places, one leg looked badly broken, as did one of his arms; the knife was gone. When he drew a breath, his chest looked caved in.

"Something is going to happen," I said. "A raid is coming. Zeppelins. Lots of them. And the bullets are no good. We need to warn the bases."

"We know about the bullets, but—"

"He said half this town was going to explode," I said, cutting the major off. "As a diversion. We need to make him tell us what that means."

The spy sputtered. Blood dripped from his mouth. "A bomb, you imbecile," he said. "And you are too late." He tried to pull the watch from his pocket, but his arms wouldn't move. "It will go off in minutes. At seven o'clock. And you can't stop it."

Then Sergeant Orr burst through the crowd. "There's a bomb, sir," he said to Major Billings. "Captain Wyman and Sergeant Dobson are heading for it."

"To do what?" I asked.

Orr looked at me, perplexed. "Defuse it, I supposed."

The spy gave a short laugh that turned into a blood-spraying sputter. "They'll not get there in time. And if they do, they'll only succeed in blowing themselves up. Any attempt to defuse it will set it off."

I felt my stomach turn to ice. Annie hugged me harder. Billings took out his watch. "It's three minutes to seven."

We held our breath and waited.

Chapter 32

Charlie

I grabbed Dobson's wrist.

"No."

"What?"

"Look at that," I said, pointing to the wires. "It's too easy. That's the first thing anyone finding this would do."

"So?"

"Well, what would James Bond do? He'd never fall for something so obvious."

"James who?"

"Never mind. Just get me a screwdriver."

I went to work on the screws, loosening them enough for Dobson the take them out the rest of the way by hand. Being newly constructed, the screws were tight, but not corroded into place. Me and Dobson had two completely out in no time.

"Two minutes," he said.

I switched to the third screw, straining until it began to turn, then twisted until it was loose enough for Dobson to take over.

"One minute and thirty seconds," he said, removing the third screw.

There was one more to go. I shoved the screwdriver at it, turned it, and stripped the screw head. No matter how hard I tried to loosen it, the flat end of the screwdriver just kept popping out of the damaged slot.

"One minute. It's no use, sir."

I dropped the screwdriver and grabbed the hammer, jamming the nail-pulling end under the lid, making a small gap.

"Grab the box," I said, as the gap widened.

"Forty-five seconds," he said, slipping his fingers under the lid.

I dropped the hammer and grabbed the lid near where his hand was, at the furthest corner from the screw. "Pull."

Our tug of war with the box widened the gap, then widened it some more.

"Thirty seconds."

The lid was at a ninety-degree angle to the box. We dropped it on the floor. Inside were wires, batteries, a sack of cordite, and another watch attached to a detonator. The watch on the outside was wired to another detonator, but without a battery, being set to go off manually if someone pulled it out. My relief was only momentary; the rest of the bomb was too complex for me to defuse. Especially not in—

"Four seconds, sir," Dobson said. I had to admire him. His voice didn't waver at all.

"Run," I said.

We raced down the corridor. Then the dim room filled with light. I heard a whoosh and felt a searing wave of heat. Instinctively, both of us dropped to the floor.

Chapter 33

Mitch

I counted the seconds, bracing myself. If Charlie hadn't found the bomb, maybe he'd be far enough away to survive the blast. If it went off prematurely, that would mean he had found it. I checked the watch: one minute to go.

The second hand ticked on. Half a minute, ten seconds, then seven o'clock came, and went. The spy frowned and cocked his head, hoping to catch the sound of an explosion, but none came.

Chapter 34

Charlie

I lifted my head. My neck felt hot, and I caught the scent of singed hair.

Dobson, still lying prone, turned his face toward me. "We're not dead?"

I got to my feet and looked back to where the bomb had been.

The box containing the bomb was still there, sitting in a large, blackened circle. The air, thick with smoke, smelled like a firing range.

"What happened?" Dobson asked, standing next to me.

"Cordite," I said. "It won't explode unless it's confined. Opening the box meant all it did was burn."

"And you knew that the explosive was cordite?"

I shrugged. "What else would it be. Come on. We need to get to the rally."

We ran out of the building, through the compound, and into the street, which was still crowded with traffic. We pushed our way into the throng and saw an army truck carrying soldiers. They weren't from our base, but they pulled us onto the back as the driver beeped and swore and revved his engine trying to get people to move out of the way.

Two minutes later, we jumped out at the edge of the sports ground and rushed through the dimming light. The soldiers spread out, braking up fights and pulling men and police officers off the women they were beating up. Then I saw Major Billings standing with a cluster of people next to a jumble of wood. We ran to them and found the major with Sergeant Orr, Annie and Mitch, and the spy. When they saw us, Mitch let go of Annie and grabbed me.

"We thought you were going to get blown up," he said, nearly crying. I held him out at arm's length. Then Annie rushed to me. "Oh, you're safe," she said, wrapping her arms around me.

"I'm fine, thanks," Sergeant Dobson said.

I extracted myself from Annie and gave him a hug. Then I turned to Major Billings. "You need to give this man a medal," I said. "I have rarely seen such calm competence under pressure."

"Well, only after you saved my life," Dobson said, looking sheepish. "So, thank you Captain, and thank Mr. Bond if you see him again."

"You defused the bomb?" Billings asked.

"Yes, sir. With Sergeant Dobsons help."

"But it was booby trapped."

"Who told you that?"

They all looked down, and I saw the spy, lying on the grass. At first, I thought he was dead, but then he opened his eyes and smiled as blood seeped from his lips. "You haven't won," he said, his voice rasping. "The bomb was a diversion. A side show. The Zeppelins are coming. You can't stop them. And you can't defeat them."

"Shows what you know," I said. "Those sabotaged bullets? We knew all about them. And we've made more. And they're being delivered as we speak. So, it's you who hasn't won."

The spy coughed, spitting blood. I thought he might die right then, but he drew a ragged breath and looked up at me. "Shows what you know. Do you think I'm working alone? Do you think we don't know what you are up to? Those bullets will never leave your base. So, it's you ..." He coughed again, spewing an alarming amount of blood. "It's you who ... who hasn't ..." Then his eyes closed.

"What did he mean?" Orr asked.

"He has confederates on the base," Billings said, "and they're going to stop the delivery."

◆

"Good work defusing that bomb," Major Billings said.

"Thank you, sir," I replied, bracing myself against the dashboard as the truck rattled down the narrow road, illuminated only by the dim glow of its headlights. Annie was next to me, one hand on the dash, the other digging into my arm as she struggled to steady herself.

"And your ruse, tricking that spy into revealing critical intelligence. Brilliant."

I felt bad about that. All I'd done was reveal top-secret information. I had no notion of the spy trying to one-up me. But Major Billings seemed to think I was some sort of super-spy, and I wasn't going to dissuade him from that opinion.

"Again, sir, thank you. But I was just doing my job."

"All Mitch did was save my life, uncle," Annie said through gritted teeth.

Billings gave no answer. He merely sped up even

225

more.

Mitch was in the back of the truck with Dobson. I knew why Billings had put Mitch back there, but Dobson hadn't done anything wrong. Quite the contrary. I guessed he was merely a victim of circumstances.

In truth, we had no idea if the spy was lying, but Major Billings was taking no chances. When he had left the base, Captain Newell was finishing up the bullets and was going to deliver them to Brody. If there were other insurgents, they would be striking soon, before Brody could fly them out.

Annie slammed into me as Billings swerved around a corner. From the back I heard a thunk and a stream of swear words. We took another corner, and I grabbed Annie to keep her from sliding into Major Billings. And all the while I stared into the darkness ahead of us, praying we wouldn't meet another vehicle. When at last, we pulled up to the gates, I realized I was still gripping Annie by the arm. I breathed a sigh of relief and let her go.

The base was lit up. All the lights were on, marking out the buildings in white light and black shadows. Major Billings said this was so Brody could take off and land, but there was no sign of the plane.

The guards opened the gate and we drove in. Major Billings stopped the truck in the middle of the field and we looked around. Everything seemed normal and calm. There were soldiers outside the hangar, and a few in front of the mess hall and offices. Major Billings slumped in his seat, took a deep breath, and blew it out.

"Lieutenant Broadmoor must have left already. That means there was no one here to stop him, or they failed. Either way—"

The revving of an engine sounded within the hangar, and moments later the plane taxied onto the field with Brody at the controls and Whittard up front in the observer's seat. Billings pulled out his pocket watch.

"He's still got time. Everything is going to plan."

The airplane gained speed, heading across the field in front of the lab. Newell, Jeffreys and Moore, stepped out of the hangar to watch. Mitch and Dobson jumped out of the back and walked toward them. Billings put the truck in gear and followed. All seemed normal. Then I saw a shadow on the lab. A dark slit that appeared and then disappeared. The door. Someone had gone in or come out. Then a figure, white in the glare of the lights, and holding a long black cylinder, dropped to the ground.

"There," I shouted, pointing.

Without comment or question, Billings hit the gas and raced forward. I kept pointing, steering him in the right direction, hoping I hadn't been imagining things. Soon, he saw it too: Private Blake, with a Lewis gun trained on the field. Billings steered toward him, crossing behind the plane as it sped along the grass. Blake saw us coming and turned the gun our way. I grabbed Annie and pulled her down, ducking as far as I could. The gun barked and bullets shattered the windshield. Annie screamed. Major Billings kept on course.

I lifted my head above the dashboard and, through the cracked window, saw Brody's airplane passing the lab. Blake swung the gun toward it. We were almost on him. Then the gun rattled. The airplane lurched to one side, and the truck slammed into the lab.

I had just enough time to brace myself against Annie, who was still stuffed down beneath the dashboard. We crashed into the wall, and I managed to smash into the foot well as Annie smashed into me. The truck shuddered; the engine stopped. Me and Annie extracted ourselves from each other. The windshield was shattered, and steam hissed from beneath the crumpled hood. Major Billings raised his head and blood flowed from a gash in his forehead. At first, I thought he'd been shot, but then I figured he must have just hit the steering wheel because he jumped out of the truck and started giving orders.

"Open the door," Annie shouted. I did, and we both tumbled out.

Mitch ran up to us and grabbed Annie. Dobson rushed past and I followed to where Private Blake was lying half underneath the truck. He wasn't dead, but he was in pretty bad shape. Dobson grabbed the Lewis gun. Billings called for medics and a stretcher, and handcuffs.

After all that had happened, the sudden calm was disconcerting. My head buzzed and the smell of exhaust and gasoline made me queasy. I looked around, unsure of what to do. Billings was pulling Blake from beneath the truck. I didn't think that was a good idea, but I wasn't going to tell him that. Dobson handed me the Lewis gun and went to help. Then Mitch and Annie were at my side, asking if I was okay.

The buzzing grew louder. I looked into the field, where the damaged plane had turned in a smooth arc and was heading our way.

"Run!"

I dropped the gun, and we raced around the truck

to where Dobson and Major Billings were still dragging Blake, and helped pull him to safety as the plane sputtered toward us, with Brody slumped over the controls and Whittard waving frantically from the observer's seat. Then it crashed into the lab right next to our truck.

The engine smashed a hole through the wall and half the plane followed it. The wings collapsed, the engine coughed and died. A cloud of oily smoke drifted through the gaping hole. We all stood, stunned by the sudden silence. In the distance, Moore, Captains Newell and Jeffreys shouted and ran toward us. Other shouts came from across the base.

I ran to the wreckage. The smoke became thicker, I could see Whittard, struggling to get out. He was just inside the lab, hemmed in by the edges of the wall and the broken bits of the wings. Brody, in the seat behind him, remained still. The part of the airplane he was sitting in looked pretty well intact, except for the line of bullet holes running down the fuselage.

I threw aside the broken shards of the wings and got to Whittard, who was struggling to get out of his seat.

"My leg," he said. "It's broken."

I grabbed his arms and pulled, and we both tumbled to the ground. Whittard screamed in pain, and I saw that his leg was bent at a gut-wrenching angle. I hoped I hadn't damaged it further, but I couldn't worry about that. I pulled him away from the lab, past Mitch and Annie who were trying to help Brody.

Then the airplane burst into flames.

Chapter 35

Mitch

I heard a roar as a fireball erupted. Then a hot blast knocked me and Annie to the ground. When I looked up, half the airplane was on fire, the flames already biting into the walls of the lab and getting closer to the truck by the second.

I went to help Annie, but she pushed me away.

"Get Brody."

Charlie dropped Whittard, who was screaming in agony, and came to help. We had nothing to climb into the cockpit with, so Charlie gave me a boost and I pulled myself up next to Brody. He was bent forward. He'd been saved from the blast by the windshield and because his head was down near the instrument panel. I shook him by the shoulder. He moaned but didn't move. Blood pooled on the floor around his feet. I tried to pull him up, but he was too heavy. Then other hands reached in. Captain Newell, Moore and another soldier, boosted up from below. We grabbed Brody and yanked him out of the pilot's seat and rushed from the fire seconds before it engulfed the rest of the plane.

We stopped a safe distance away and laid Brody, Whittard, and Blake on the grass while the soldiers went to get stretchers. Major Billings told Captain Jeffreys to find a doctor and ordered anyone with medical training to do what they could for Brody and Whittard. He didn't mention Blake.

Then the truck exploded, sending a geyser of smoke, fire and debris into the air. We dropped to the ground as bits of wood and metal fell around us. When the last of it settled, we started to get up, then dropped again as the ammunition in the airplane began to go off. Tracer bullets popped and whizzed into the air, zinging over our heads as we tried to sink as low as possible into the short grass.

Moments later, the stretcher bearers arrived, crawling on the ground, dragging the stretchers behind them, as if they were on a battlefield. Brody lay still. The medics had done what they could about the hole in his leg but had been unable to look for other wounds because he was clutching his arms around his chest so tightly. As they moved him to the stretcher, he opened his eyes and looked around until he saw me.

"Lieutenant Wyman," he said, unfolding his arms. "I have something for you." Inside his flight jacket, lying on his chest, was an ammunition pan. "I had it with me ... to deliver in person. Take it to Sutton's Farm. It's for Willy Robinson ... you remember?

His breathing came harder, and he closed his eyes. Billings grabbed the pan and told the stretcher bearers to move on.

Still lying on the ground, Billings held the pan out toward me.

"You heard him."

"But ..." Where did I start? It was dark. I'd never find the base on my own, and I was sure to crash land if I did.

I never got the chance the make my excuses, or

231

take the ammunition because, just then, another pan went off. When I looked up again, I saw Billings shaking his head.

"Everything depends on it," he said, "You have to try."

That didn't make me feel any better, and neither did the answer Capitan Newell gave when a soldier asked him how many ammunition pans were in the airplane.

"I loaded a dozen, so counting that one, and—"

Another pan exploded, then another.

"About eight more, I should think."

We crawled, then ran, after the stretcher bearers, and almost made it to the buildings when the lab lit up in a huge fire ball. Blinding light and searing heat hit us as the night turned into the brightest day I had ever seen. Everyone hit the ground again. I pulled Annie down and we lay flat, my face in the grass as a wave of heat rolled over my back. The flare-up died out in a few moments, and we cautiously climbed to our feet. The lab was fully engulfed now, with yellow and green and blue flames shooting into the sky and the smell of oily smoke in the air.

"The chemicals," Captain Newell said, referring to the strange colours of the flames. "And that flare-up, that was the cordite burning. The worst of it is over now."

Then more ammunition began to explode. It wasn't the incendiary bullets, so I couldn't see them, but I heard whizzing overhead and all around us. The explosions threw hunks of burning wood into the air, setting other buildings on fire. All we could do was watch; no one wanted to run into the field with a bucket of water with all those bullets flying around.

If the exploding ammunition in the airplane made it seem like a battle, this made it seem like a war. Hot metal and glowing embers fell from the sky, fires burned, bullets whizzed, munitions exploded. We crept along the ground toward the barracks door, which was already pockmarked with bullet holes, making me wonder how much safer we were going to be inside.

More buildings caught fire. Another explosion, then a loud "pop," and all the lights went out, turning the bright white into flickering yellow.

"The generators," Billings said. "This is going to make things even worse."

Then Moore shouted, "The hangar's on fire!"

I turned and saw flames sprouting from the roof and edging toward the walls.

"Move, men," Billings said. "We have to get the other plane out."

Leaving the pan of ammunition on the ground, he jumped up and ran toward the hangar. The others, even Charlie, ran after him. I told Annie to stay where she was and followed.

I've seen movies where they try to show how scary it was fighting in World War One, and how they had to go "over the top," which meant climbing out of the safety of their trenches and running straight into enemy machine gun fire. Let me tell you, those movies never came close. It was terrifying. Bullets zinged all around me. Fires, explosions, men screaming, some falling, and all of us running toward the hangar, which was becoming engulfed in flames.

By the time we got there, it was too hot to go inside to push the plane out. Bits of the roof began falling in and the back of the hangar was burning. We tried to rush in, to get behind the wings, but the heat drove us back. The fire grew, and Moore shouted that the petrol in the barrels could explode at any moment. Bullets pounded into the side of the hangar. We ducked and waited, feeling exposed and helpless. Then, from behind, someone shouted:

"We need to pull it out, not push it. Get a rope. Tie it to the propeller. Quick!"

I turned and saw Annie rushing toward us. I ran and tackled her.

"What do you think you're doing?" I asked.

She pushed me off and tried to get up while I tried to hold her down.

"You didn't think I was going to let you get killed without me," she said, struggling to stand again.

I caught the hem of her dress and pulled. It didn't make her fall, but the fabric ripped away, revealing her strangely ample underwear. She stopped and glared at me with an expression of shock and anger. So, I grabbed her leg and tripped her.

"I told you to stay where it was safe."

She twisted away. "I don't take orders from you, but if you don't want me with you then, fine, I'll just go back where I came from."

She tried to stand, and I pulled her down again, pinning her to the ground. She started hitting me, but I held tight.

"I don't want to see you hurt," I said between punches. "I don't think I could take that."

"Well, I don't want to see you get hurt, either" she said, still punching me. Then she pulled me to her, kissed me and started to cry. "Don't get killed," she said. "Promise."

"I promise I'll try."

"You'll do it," she said, kissing me again. "You won't try."

"Break it up, will you," Charlie shouted, "and come help us."

Charlie and Moore had looped a rope around the propeller and everyone else was pulling on it like they were in a big, one-sided tug-o-war. Annie and I grabbed the end of the rope and heaved. We strained, digging our heels into the dirt, pulling with all our strength. The plane began to move, inching forward, rolling slowly out of the burning building.

The soldier in front of me screamed and fell, gripping his side. We kept pulling. Bullets pounded into the side of the airplane. I pulled harder, hoping it had not sustained too much damage. Then the petrol tanks exploded, sending a wave of smoke, fire and embers gushing from the open doors. We kept pulling, as the hangar collapsed into a flaming heap, moving the airplane as far from the burning buildings as we could. When we got far enough away, we all hit the ground again as the bullets continued to whiz around us. The fires burned brighter, but there were fewer explosions. We kept our heads down and waited.

After a few minutes, the popping tapered off and Moore went to examine the plane. Major Billings ran to his office and the rest of us helped the stretcher bearers comb the field for wounded soldiers. We still had to duck occasionally, but soon, whatever was going to explode had exploded, and the only sound was the roar of the fires.

We carried the wounded to the mess hall, which we turned into a temporary hospital. The soldiers scrounged up lanterns and candles for light, and cloth for bandages, and soon Captain Jeffreys arrived with a doctor and half a dozen nurses. He had driven into town in the only vehicle he could salvage from the Motor Pool, and had found no shortage of volunteers, though he could only cram so many into the car. They set to work, and Annie, Charlie and I helped out as best we could. Then Major Billings returned and called me over to a table in the corner. Charlie and Annie (now dressed in a khaki private's uniform) came with me. Billings and Captain Newell were already at the table waiting for us. They looked grim.

"I've just received news over the radio," Billings said. "The Zeppelins are on their way; it's the largest raid so far. Unfortunately, the pilots from the other bases have already taken off, with the sabotaged ammunition. There is no way we can get that one good pan to any of them on time."

It must have been devastating for him to admit that because the ramifications were dire. Even so (and I struggled hard to hide it) I felt nothing but relief, because I was pretty sure I couldn't do it. I'd have crashed trying to land, or gotten lost, then crashed. The outcome of me doing my bit to deliver the ammunition would be the same if I didn't do anything, only I'd still be alive. Then I noticed that Billings and Captain Newell were still staring at me with a mixture of resignation and pity.

"However," Billings said, clearing his throat, "we do have a plan. Flight Sergeant Moore is confident he can patch up the observer aircraft. It is damaged, but air-worthy. It will be ready to fly within the hour."

"But," I said, my stomach sinking, "if it's too late to deliver the bullets, what good will that do?"

Billings looked at me, and then at Charlie. "Lieutenant Huntington assures me you are a capable pilot, Captain Wyman is proficient with the Lewis gun, and we have procured three drums of Pomeroy ammunition from one of the undamaged stores. You will fly the plane and find a Zeppelin. Captain Wyman will use the explosive ammunition to punch a hole in it, then use the new bullets to set it on fire. We only need one kill to assure the Government, and the population, that all is not lost. And you are our only hope."

When he finished speaking, everyone around the table kept silent. My sinking stomach turned to ice and threatened to make an appearance on the tabletop.

"That's an insane plan," Annie said.

I was grateful for that because it was exactly what I was thinking. However, Major Billings didn't change his expression. He didn't even look at her. He just shook his head and locked his eyes on mine.

"We will give you a trajectory to follow for the best chance of interception. The night is clear, so the odds of spotting one will be high. Once you find a target, engage."

A trickle of sweat ran down my back. "The observation plane, it has no weapons, how—"

"Flight Sergeant Moore will fit the observer's seat with a Lewis gun."

"What about the excess weight? With a Lewis gun and an extra man, the fuel won't last long."

Billings sighed. "It will last long enough to get you there."

"What about getting back?" Charlie asked. Again, I was grateful; it was a question my mouth was too dry to ask.

But no answer came. Billings lowered his eyes and Newell looked at the table, and I understood that we weren't expected to return.

Chapter 36
Sunday, 3 September 1916

Mitch

We took off just after midnight.

Moore helped me and Charlie into our flight gear—leather helmets, goggles, silk scarfs, leather jackets, and heavy leather gloves—and walked us out to the airplane as if he were leading us to a firing squad. They had removed the duplicate set of controls from the observer's seat and added a Lewis gun, loaded with a pan of Pomeroy bullets. The final pan of unadulterated incendiary bullets had been loaded into the cockpit, along with the two spare Pomeroy pans. The airplane's fuel tank had been topped-up with petrol they had scrounged from everywhere in the base that wasn't on fire, and Moore told us he was confident that, even with the combined weight of me, Charlie, and the Lewis gun, we could still get three hours of flight time. More or less.

Major Billings and Captain Newell waited by the airplane. Annie was there too, and when she saw me, she grabbed me in a hug so tight it squeezed the breath out of me.

"Don't do this," she said, her face buried in the front of my coat. "You can't, you can't."

I hugged her back and let her sob a while, then

gently pried her off.

"Remember when you first met me," I said. "You gave me a white feather because you wanted me to go to the front lines. That's what I'm doing now."

"But I didn't love you then," she said. "I didn't know that, if you died, I'd die with you."

"You won't," I said. "Look here." I pulled the feather she had given me from my pocket. "I'm keeping this with me. For luck, and to keep you close."

"I'm so ashamed," she said, wiping her face with my scarf. "I called you a coward, and you're the bravest man I know. And it was wrong, I was wrong. Even if I wasn't in love with you, someone else might have been. You'd have had a sweetheart, a mother, a sister, someone whose heart would break if you …"

I hugged her tight. "None of that matters now. All that matters is, I have to do this. We have to do this."

For the first time, she looked at Charlie.

"Oh, Charlie," she said, wrapping her arms around him, "I'm so sorry I got you into this."

Charlie gave her an awkward pat and pushed her away.

"Annie," Billings said, "it's time. They need to go."

Annie kissed me again. I held her close and whispered, "I love you. And nothing will ever change that."

I climbed onto the wing and into the pilot's seat, followed by Charlie, who settled into the observer's cockpit behind me. I put on my gloves. Moore tugged the propeller. The engine caught and rumbled to life.

"Don't die," Annie shouted over the engine's roar. "Stay alive. Whatever it takes, stay alive. Promise me that."

"I will," I shouted, then waved, and taxied onto the field.

The plane trundled over the ground as I began my take-off. There was ample light from the fires, but it wasn't static, like a floodlight. It flickered and the shadows danced, and I hoped all the wounded soldiers had been taken from the field because I couldn't be sure of seeing them. Then the plane bumped and jumped and sailed into the air. We climbed over the fires and the perimeter fence, into the night sky, and I felt so free that, for a moment, I forgot what was ahead of us.

Away from the heat of the fires it grew suddenly colder, and the higher we flew the colder it got. I set a northeasterly course and continued to climb. Below and behind I could still see the glowing flames from the base, and I used that as a reference point to keep me headed in the right direction to intercept the Zeppelins. I settled in and eased the airplane higher. It was going to take a long time to get to ten thousand feet, and even then, there was little chance of finding anything in the endless, black sky.

When we approached the area our intelligence suggested the Zeppelins would be, I turned toward London. With a blackout in place, there wasn't much to suggest there was a huge city below, but the surface of the Thames wound like a silver snake across the dark landscape. That would be where the Zeppelins were heading. I flew in a big circle but found nothing. The few lights on the ground shrank to pinpoints mimicking the stars in the dark sky, and below, wispy clouds reflected light from the crescent moon. Still, I saw no Zeppelins. An hour came and went, offering nothing but endless black. I was beginning to think I was simply going to fly in circles until the petrol ran out and we crashed.

I started climbing higher, hoping we'd have better luck at eleven thousand feet. I was watching the altimeter and compass on the instrument panel when, over the drone of the engine, Charlie shouted.

"The stars," he said. "They're disappearing."

I looked up and saw I was flying toward a hole in the sky; a hole that appeared to be growing. There wasn't anything there, just a hole, as if the stars were being swallowed up. In moments, the entire sky turned an inky black, and I realized what was happening. I pulled back on the stick, sending the airplane nearly straight up into the sky. It wasn't a hole; it was a Zeppelin.

The force of the climb pressed me into the seat, and I struggled to keep control. The plane continued to climb. I held my breath, expecting to crash into the Zeppelin at any moment. Then, with feet to spare, it passed underneath us. Easing the stick forward, I levelled out and flew along its length. It wasn't big, it was enormous, as vast as the sky itself. It passed with surprising speed, and yet we had still not reached the tail. We continued along its length, wondering what to do. Then someone started shooting at us.

I looked down and saw a small platform on top of the Zeppelin holding German soldiers, and a machine gun. I wrenched the stick to the right, then left, and then flew down the side of the Zeppelin, out of their line of fire where, incredibly, I saw another airplane.

It was a Night Fighter, heading away from us. The pilot was shooting his Lewis gun at the Zeppelin, strafing the side while machine guns fired back. Tracer bullets zoomed through the air and muzzle-flashes from the machine guns lit up, revealing several firing positions on the underside of the Zeppelin. I flew away from the fight and circled back, tracking the Night Fighter from a distance, staying out of sight and, I hoped, out of range.

The Zeppelin appeared to be trying to lose the Night Fighter, heading fast in a northerly direction. But the pilot wasn't deterred. He turned and chased the Zeppelin, readying for another pass. Then I saw its markings. It was Lieutenant Robinson, the pilot I was supposed to have given the only good ammunition pan to. That's because Brody thought he was the best, but he was using the ammunition wrong. He wasn't supposed to strafe, he was supposed to shoot into the same place. I watched in helpless frustration as he turned and made another strafing run.

"What's he doing?" Charlie shouted from behind me.

I didn't answer; I kept an eye on Robinson, who had turned in preparation for another attack. I thought about flying close to him to shout instructions about how to use his ammunition. I knew that could never work, however, so I dove and turned and came up behind him as he prepared to fire.

It looked like he was going to strafe the side again, but instead he flew directly at the rear of the airship and, when he got close, he fired straight into it, pouring all his bullets into a single spot. If Farber had not tampered with his bullets, he would have succeeded. Although the Pomeroy bullets worked as expected—blowing a large opening in the Zeppelin's skin—the incendiary bullets mixed with the Pomeroys merely flared and died, not even reaching their mark.

243

Robinson arced away from the Zeppelin, flying downward to increase his speed and to get out of the range of the machine guns that continued to fire at him.

That must have been his last pan, because he continued his dive and did not return.

I kept my eye on the spot Robinson had shot at.

"Charlie," I shouted. "Get ready."

Chapter 37

Charlie

I couldn't believe how boring flying was. Boring, cold, and uncomfortable. After the bone-rattling take-off, and getting over the feeling that the plane was going to fall out of the sky, all I could do was settle back and wait. It took an hour to climb up to where Mitch said the Zeppelins were, and the higher we got the more I appreciated my leather gear and goggles. I was cold, but not freezing, though my cheeks were raw. The only interesting thing that happened was, an hour into the flight I discovered why pilots wore silk scarves: it wasn't just for warmth, it also keeps your neck from getting chaffed while you constantly twist your head every which-way.

It's amazing how big the sky is. And at night, you can't see anything, and you can't hear anything because of the roar of the engine. It was hopeless. We'd been told there were Zeppelins out there, and I had been told they were plenty big, but the sky was bigger, and they seemed to be able to hide in the dark.

I was getting bored and frustrated, and I didn't want to waste a suicide mission doing nothing but flying around for hours finding nothing to shoot at. Then I noticed we were flying toward a hole in the sky. It looked like the stars were disappearing, so I shouted to Mitch, and watched as it grew bigger and bigger, until I was suddenly slammed into my seat as Mitch went into a vertical climb and the Zeppelin passed beneath us.

The biggest thing I had ever seen up till then was a jet airliner, and I had thought that was immense, but to the Zeppelin, the airliner was just a toy. It was like an island in the sky, or a lake, big enough to have islands in it. And, as I scanned its surface, I saw it really did have an island in it, and it was inhabited by four German soldiers and one machine gun. As soon as they saw us, they started firing, and I got to test the limits of my harness as Mitch zigged and zagged and dove over the side of the Zeppelin. That's when I saw the other airplane.

It was one of the planes Mitch calls a Night Fighter, strafing the side of the Zeppelin just like the pilots were told not to do. I smacked my forehead with the palm of my hand and shook my head, willing the guy to smarten up.

Mitch flew away from the Zeppelin and circled back in time to see the pilot doing a second strafing run. What an idiot. Still, we followed him, and on his third try he, at last, flew straight at the Zeppelin, firing his Lewis gun into a single spot in front of him. The Pomeroy bullets worked, blowing a big hole in the Zeppelin's thin skin. But the glow from the tainted incendiary rounds winked out before they got near the target. As the spy had promised, the bullets were useless.

Watching the pilot attacking the Zeppelin, I could see why they weren't keen on doing what we asked. By the time all the rounds had been fired, the pilot was really close and, not only were the Germans shooting at him, he was also flying straight into their guns. Somehow, he survived. The pilot, having done all he could, took a sharp turn and disappeared into the dark.

Then Mitch levelled the airplane. "Charlie," he said. "Get ready."

"Get what ready?"

"The bullets. I'm going to fly to the hole the pilot made. Shoot into it."

He was already flying toward the Zeppelin, but I needed to change the pan. The one mounted on the Lewis gun was filled with Pomeroy bullets. The Night Fighter pilot had wisely mixed the rounds in his pan, but mine were all a single type. I yanked the pan off the Lewis gun and searched for the one Newell had filled and, thankfully, clearly labelled. I attempted to slot the new pan onto the gun, but it proved awkward while wearing the bulky gloves, so I pulled them off. They flew out of the cockpit, and immediately my fingers went numb.

As the feeling left my hands, I attached the drum. After it clicked into place, I blew on my hands to get some feeling in them, grabbed the Lewis gun and swivelled it around to aim at the Zeppelin. Being in the rear seat, I couldn't point the gun straight ahead and, instead, had to aim a little to the side.

"Get close," I shouted, hoping Mitch could hear, "then turn slightly right to give me a shot."

He raised a gloved hand with his thumb pointing up to show he understood. I held tight and waited. I had forty-seven bullets and I only needed to hit the target area with one, so it was a sure bet. The air was calm, the airplane was steady. I looked down the site of the Lewis gun. The Zeppelin loomed closer.

Then spots of light blinked from the underside of

the Zeppelin. Bullets whizzed around us, and I heard the rattle of machine guns. Mitch jerked the airplane to the right. I squeezed the trigger. The gun jolted and the force of the turn slammed me against the side of the cockpit, causing me to pull the stock of the Lewis gun down and point the barrel straight up. My frozen fingers held the trigger, spraying the incendiary rounds in a long arc over the top of the Zeppelin while machine gun bullets thudded into the side of the airplane.

"Get us out of here," I shouted.

"Hang on," Mitch shouted in return.

We banked sharply as the German guns kept pounding us and the Lewis gun spit lines of blue light into the night. Then everything went silent, or as silent as it can get in an open-top airplane.

My heart pounded. I drew several deep breaths, pried my hands from the Lewis gun, and tried to not think about how I had fired forty-seven rounds at a Zeppelin the size of an ocean liner and had not only missed the area I'd been aiming for, I had also missed the Zeppelin. Mitch said nothing, but he was probably thinking the same thing: we had failed.

"There's no sense hanging around here," he said. "We still have a little fuel left. I'll head back south. Maybe we can find a place to land before we run out."

I nodded, knowing he couldn't see or hear me, but not caring. If we did manage to land, I'd have to explain how I had failed so spectacularly, and I thought maybe crashing wouldn't be so bad after all. I stuffed my hands into my pockets to try to thaw them out. Then a warmth spread through my chest.

"Turn around," I shouted, "back to the Zeppelin."

"What for? There's no ammunition left."

I pulled the bullet out of my pocket, the bullet granddad had sent us, the bullet I had secretly charged, and said to Mitch: "No. We still have one left."

◆

Mitch turned back toward the Zeppelin. I pulled the empty pan off the Lewis gun and took the bullet out of my pocket. As I tried to slot it in, the airplane lurched.

"They're shooting at us," Mitch said, sending the plane into a wild zig-zag.

"Straighten up. I need more time," I said, and dropped the bullet, and the pan.

They rolled around by my feet as the airplane shifted one way, then the other. I strained to reach them, but couldn't, and I saw the bullet was in danger of slipping through one of the cracks in the cockpit floor. I unstrapped myself and dove for it, grabbing it in my fist as the airplane lurched again. Still crouched low in the cockpit, I jammed the bullet into the pan. Then I reached up and put the pan on the Lewis gun, praying that Mitch didn't throw me off with another sudden manoeuvre.

I strapped myself in, took the handles of the Lewis gun and swivelled it into position. Mitch swerved right and left and up and down to avoid the machine guns. Bullets whizzed around us. The Zeppelin grew larger and larger as we neared. Mitch pulled to the right and, suddenly, the side of the Zeppelin was right in front of me. The area the pilot had shot into drifted into sight, a patch of dark on the grey skin of the Zeppelin where the Pomeroy bullets had blown a hole in it and, hopefully, the gas bags inside. I aimed the Lewis gun and pulled the trigger.

A blue streak shot toward the Zeppelin, straight into the black hole. I shouted for Mitch to get us away and, even as he turned, I saw a flash of light from inside the Zeppelin. We dove, putting us in full view of the Zeppelin's machine guns. We were diving and gaining speed, but not enough. The bullets whizzed around us. I saw holes appear in the wing. More machine guns joined in, and more bullets came our way.

Then I heard a rumble, like close thunder., and the sky behind us lit up, and the bullets stopped flying. A wave of hot air caught us, sending the airplane tumbling end over end. I saw stars, blackness, and then a huge ball of yellow flame as fire spread through the Zeppelin. Then stars, black, and another glimpse of the Zeppelin, now sinking with the burning end down. More gas bags exploded, but we were far enough away now.

The airplane settled into a spinning dive, gaining speed. I shook the dizziness from my head and shouted for Mitch. He didn't answer. Below, pinpoints of light spun crazily. I didn't know how far away they were, but they were getting closer. The plane began to shudder.

"Mitch," I shouted, but he didn't answer. Then I remembered something from just before we took off. "Your promise," I said. "You promised Annie you would stay alive. No matter what it took."

Chapter 38

Mitch

I felt cold, tired, and sick. Everything was black. My head spun. Then I heard Annie's name. Then I opened my eyes to the sting of cold air and saw lights swirling below and felt the shuddering of the airplane and knew we were crashing.

But we hadn't crashed yet, and I had promised Annie to stay alive.

I pulled back on the stick, just a little, and stabilized the airplane so it stopped spinning. Then I eased the stick back again. The airplane began to pull out of the dive, but the force pushed me so hard into my seat that I knew it would break the airplane apart, so I eased back.

Slowly, I pulled the nose of the airplane level. The wings stopped vibrating and the engine settled into a steady rhythm. Beneath the plane, trees—black in the night—zipped by. I climbed to gain more altitude. Way behind us, the burning Zeppelin remained visible, still sinking slowly to the ground. I used it as a marker and set a course south. We had flown north-northeast, then northwest to just beyond London, so south seemed a good bet.

Truth was, I had no idea where we were or how to get back to base. Or how much fuel we had.

"Throw everything out that's not nailed down," I

said. "The lighter we are, the longer we can stay in the air."

He said nothing, but I heard him rummaging around.

"One empty pan," he said. "Three loaded Pomeroy pans." Then, after a few grunts. "One Lewis gun." Some loud banging and an ominous crack. "One Lewis gun bracket."

"That's enough," I said, worried he might throw his seat out next.

I climbed higher and watched the lights of London ease by, followed by the dark of the countryside. There were a few lights scattered over the hills and fields, and occasionally a town or a village, but they didn't do us any good. I needed a flat place to land and, in the dark, I couldn't tell a pasture from a forest, not until it was too late.

I scanned the blackness below for signs of an airfield, a military base or even a town park that might be lit up at two-thirty in the morning. I didn't bother looking for our base. I knew it didn't have any lights.

All I could do was fly in a straight line south. If we made it to the coast, we could ditch in the water. But the coast was still a long way off and I doubted we could get that far. In truth, I was surprised we still had any fuel left. Then, as if the plane had read my mind, the engine sputtered and died, and the night went suddenly silent.

The plane glided through the air with just the whoosh of the wind in my ears.

"What are we going to do?" Charlie asked from behind.

"We're going to have to glide," I said, not wanting to tell him it was hopeless. "When we get close to the ground, we'll look for a place to land."

In the daylight, with a clear, level field in front of us, it was possible. I had seen Brody do it once, but I had never tried it. I didn't bother telling Charlie that, however. I just told him to keep looking for an open area.

I kept the airplane in as smooth a glide as I could, maintaining maximum altitude without stalling. It was tricky and required concentration, so I wasn't happy when Charlie started shouting at me.

"The base," he said. "Over there. That's our base."

"It can't be. There is no way you could pick out our base."

"I can," he insisted. "Look over there. It's a light."

He was right, there was a light, but that didn't mean anything.

"That's probably just a house," I said, "or a village. There won't be anywhere to land."

"It's not a village. Fly toward it. Keep your eyes on it. You'll see."

There was no dissuading him, so I turned the plane and headed toward the light. We had enough altitude to get there, but when we did, we'd probably crash into the forest.

Then I noticed something. It was different from the lights of the big towns we had flown over.

"See," Charlie said. "It flickers, like a fire."

"But that doesn't necessarily mean—"

"Keep watching," Charlie said.

The plane was slowing. I had to sacrifice more altitude to keep it from stalling, altitude we couldn't get back. Chasing the light was suicidal.

"You're going to get us killed," I said, thinking, "sooner rather than later."

"Just keep watching," Charlie said.

Then the flickering light fared and, for a second, turned blue.

"That's our base," Charlie said again. "It's still burning. The chemicals are making the fire change colour."

My heart began to race. He was right. It had to be our base. I levelled the plane and prayed we had enough altitude.

The light loomed closer, the ground drew nearer, and the air grew warmer. The smell of engine oil from the airplane mixed with the scents of smoke and burning chemicals. Aiming for the base meant a steeper glide and now the ground began to zip by way too fast. I pulled back, easing our speed by climbing, then dipped again to keep from stalling.

The perimeter fence came into view. If I held steady and the plane didn't slow, I could clear it and, hopefully, avoid the wreckage of the hangar. In the field, silhouetted by the still-burning lab, were half a dozen people. And I was heading straight toward them.

The night was dark, the plane was silent, so there was no way they would hear us, and no way to warn them. Who were they? One looked like Billings. Was that Newell? And Annie? Was she there? Annie was carrying a small sack, walking with the others along the path I would need to land on. I had a choice: crash before I got to them, or run them down, and I had seconds to make it.

"What are you doing?" Charlie shouted as the plane cleared the fence and I dove toward the hangar.

I had no time to answer. I levelled the plane as the wheels hit the collapsed roof, sending a shower of sparks into the air. The smouldering wood splintered with a grating sound as the plane lurched and swooped toward the group. But the sound had alerted them. They turned, saw the plane, and scattered, shouting and diving into the grass.

The plane touched down where they had been, too fast and too sharply. I tried to pull up, but the wheels slammed onto the ground. With a crack, the undercarriage broke, and the airplane thudded on the hard-packed earth. We skidded until the propeller dug into the dirt, then flipped over, and everything went dark.

Chapter 39
Monday, 4 September 1916

Mitch

When I woke, I had an aching head, a dry mouth, and a bandage on my arm. The room was dim, but through the dirty windows I could see it was light outside. There were four other beds in the room, lined up along one wall. Charlie, who was sitting up reading a book, was in the one to my left. In the bed to my right—his leg in traction, propped up with pillows, and smoking his pipe—was Brody. The other bed was empty, but sleeping in a nearby chair was Annie, still wearing her rumpled khaki.

"Good morning," Charlie said, glancing over the top of his book. "Thought you'd sleep the day away." He tilted his head, indicating a clock on the far wall that read three fifteen. Since it wasn't dark outside, I assumed it was late in the afternoon.

Brody took the pipe out of his mouth. "Ah, the hero awakes."

I tried to sit up. My head spun and I became aware that, unlike Charlie who was wearing his informal uniform, I had on some sort of loose nightgown. Brody, true to form, was in a silk dressing gown, royal blue with maroon trim.

Through the windows in the wall facing me, I could see the smouldering ruins of the base, and soldiers scurrying back and forth with wheelbarrows and shovels. Incredibly, in the midst of the activity, standing on crutches and with his leg in a cast, was Whittard. Moore was next to him, and they were both shouting orders to the soldiers.

Behind them was the ruined plane, and I wondered if they were going to try to rebuild it. Brody saw me looking. "Hell of a thing, what? The base getting bombed by a Zeppelin and all that?" Then he winked at me.

Annie woke up then and gasped when she saw me.

"You're awake," she said, running toward me, and slapping Brody's good leg on the way. "Why didn't you wake me?" Then she threw herself on me, sobbing and laughing at the same time. "Oh, thank God, you're awake."

I hugged her awkwardly with my good arm. "Ouch!"

"Oh, sorry. I forgot. You're hurt."

She wrapped her arms around my neck and kissed me.

"Now, now, Miss McAllister," Brody said. "Let's demonstrate some decorum."

"Shove it, Brody," Annie said, her face still buried in my neck.

Brody shook his head in mock disgust. "Tsk, tsk. I expected better from you."

"I taught her that," Charlie said, turning another page in his book.

Annie eased off, then, and pulled away, looking down at me with shining eyes. "Thank you for not giving up."

I shook my head. "It was more luck than anything."

"No, Captain Wyman," Brody said. "It was your excellent flying, and young Miss McAllister's faith that saved you."

"Captain?"

"Yes," Brody said. "Another promotion."

"But how can you promote me above your rank?"

"I didn't. Major Billings did."

"He's forgiven me, then?"

Annie snorted. "You saved my life. He should have given you a medal for that. Instead, he sent you on a suicide mission. But you came back, so he had to promote you."

"You're evens now, by the way," Charlie said.

"That's right," Brody said. "After you left, Major Billings assumed he'd never see you again, and he was going to leave it at that. But Miss McAllister wouldn't hear of it. She demanded that they not put out the fires. In fact, she made her Uncle Henry order his soldiers to dismantle the undamaged buildings to feed the blazing lab. Then, when they found a store of redundant chemicals, she came up with the idea of throwing them on the fire to make it flare up and show different colours. She knew if you saw that, you'd realize you were near the base."

I looked at Annie. "You … you're amazing." Then she kissed me again.

"She portioned the chemicals into bags," Charlie said, "then waited until she thought you might be coming back and started throwing the bags into the fire at ten-minute intervals. They were taking the last bag to the fire when you almost ran them down."

I didn't know what to say, so I just hugged her and forgot about the pain.

Then the door opened, and Major Billings entered.

Annie let me go and stood next to the bed, as if at attention. Behind Major Billings was a man in a dark suit and bowler hat. He had a round face and— apparent when he took off his hat—thinning red hair. He strode into the room as if he owned it, and had the look of a man of much importance, or at least much importance as far as he was concerned. When he saw Brody, he went to his bedside.

"Young Broadmoor," he said, shaking his hand, "I see the Hun hasn't finished you off yet. Tell me, how are your father's roses this season?"

"They are doing fine. He's developed a new hybrid. You must come and see them. Bring your paints."

They spoke a few minutes more about nothing in particular, then the man stepped to the centre of the room, looked from Charlie to me to Annie to Brody, and said:

"You will all, of course, sign the Official Secrets Act."

"What's that?" Charlie asked.

"Something you will sign to prohibit you from talking about anything that has happened here, or revealing what I am about to tell you."

"And if we don't?"

"Men will come to your home, take you away, and no one will ever hear from you again."

Charlie shrugged. "Fair enough."

"First," the man continued, "I must commend you on your bravery. Even you, private McAllister." At this he nodded to Annie and gave her a wink. "Your bravery will be rewarded, but what you have done must never be known. Our country needs a hero, and Lieutenant William Leefe-Robinson will be better

259

received, and believed, than two young Canadians. The Government has already decided to give Lieutenant Robinson a Victoria Cross, and the official report will show that he brought down the Zeppelin unaided."

The man looked as if he thought we might be angry about that.

"But he deserves the credit," I said.

"Yeah," Charlie said. "All we did was shoot the bullets that he should have had in the first place. Without him, it wouldn't have happened."

The man nodded, seemingly satisfied. "Later today, Government officials will pay you a visit, bringing papers to sign and medals to bestow on you that you cannot talk about or show to anyone. Is that clear?"

We all nodded, including Major Billings, who had stood silently behind the man all this time.

"Very good, then. And I was never here."

We nodded at that, and expected the man to leave, but he stayed where he was, looking a little bit awkward, as if he wanted to tell us more, but wasn't sure if he should. Then Brody broke the silence.

"Is there any other news," he asked, "that might be of interest?"

The man broke into a self-satisfied grin. "Since you asked, you may be wondering why a disgraced backbencher has been sent on such an important mission."

I had to admit I didn't. I also didn't know what a backbencher was, and I didn't consider what he was doing was very important, but I didn't tell him that.

"There is," the man continued in a conspiratorial tone, "going to be a change in the government soon and, if all goes to plan, I will become the Minister of Munitions."

I wasn't sure what that was, either, but he seemed to think it was something important.

"Congratulations," Brody said. "That's a step in the right direction."

I shook my head and looked out the window again. Whittard and Moore were now inspecting the wrecked observer, pointing at broken bits and likely planning how they could fix it to be better than before. Then I had a thought.

"If you are to become the Minister of Munitions," I said, "then perhaps you'd like to get a look at some new ideas."

The man turned to me, his brow furrowed. "I would, indeed."

"The airplane I flew last night. It's been modified by Flight Sergeant Moore and Air Mechanic First Class Whittard. Without those innovation, I would not have been able to do what I'm not supposed to say we did. They are outside now, inspecting the wreckage of the aircraft."

The man turned toward the windows, then looked back at me. "I shall do that. Thank you, Captain."

After thanking us one last time, he and Billings left. As soon as the door closed, Annie settled on the bed next to me. Through the window, I saw Billings lead the man directly to the ruined airplane, where he shook hands with Whittard and Moore.

"Who was that?" Charlie asked.

Brody waved a hand dismissively. "A friend of the family," he said. "A political opportunist, always in search of a favourable wind, nobody of real importance."

261

"His name?" Charlie asked.

Brody drew on his pipe. "Winston," he said. "Winston Churchill. But don't bother remembering his name. He'll never amount to much."

Chapter 40
Tuesday, 5 September 1916

Charlie

We left the base the following morning.

After saying good-bye to everyone, Major Billings drove us to Horsham in the only automobile left in the Motor Pool. I sat up front, while Mitch and Annie sat in back and Major Billings tried to avoid looking over his shoulder every two seconds.

Along the way, I heard Annie ask Mitch to tell her all about the cloak and his adventures and how Maggie knew us, and he told her. I wasn't sure if that was a good idea or not, but there was nothing I could do about it. Besides, she'd signed the Official Secrets Act, and we were part of it, so it wasn't like she could tell anyone. And even if she did, no one would believe her.

I think that was part of the reason she wanted to hear it from Mitch. Believing something is true is different than knowing something is true, and I think she was hoping that Mitch telling our story would help her know.

When we got to Horsham. Major Billings parked the car, and we walked to Maggie's, where things got a lot more family-like and less military-like.

We dressed in civilian clothes, Annie gave her torn dress to Maggie for mending, changed out of her khaki, and we all sat down to a big lunch of boiled vegetables, ham, and homemade bread, as if we were a normal family. After lunch, Maggie said it was time, and the five of us set out for the Shaw farm.

Frank Shaw was not in when we arrived. Agnes welcomed us, Edith beamed, and Verdy—still wrapped in our cloak—gurgled. Frank came in shortly after, having seen us enter the farmyard from the barn where he'd been working. He'd come ready to get some answers out of us, or turn us over to the authorities, but the sight of Major Billings calmed him down, as did Maggie's promise that everything would soon be made clear.

Agnes gave us our clothes and, after changing, we returned to the kitchen where everyone, except Maggie and Edith (and, of course, Verdy), stared in amazement.

"That's how you dress where you come from?" Annie asked.

Mitch shrugged. "It's not so different."

We walked in silence to the burned-out house. Some attempts had been made to clear the site; not much, but enough that we could get to the central fireplace, with its soot-blackened chimney that loomed like a sentry, guarding the wreckage, and the hearth in front of it, where we had appeared nearly two weeks before.

"This is good-bye, then," Annie said, holding Mitch's hand and staring into the ruin. "You'll need your cloak. Is that how it works?"

Mitch nodded. Frank and Major Billings both looked like they had questions, but Maggie waved a hand at them, and they stayed quiet.

I turned to Edith, who was still holding Verdy. I

stroked the sleeping baby's forehead, then laid my hand on the cloak. "We need that back now," I said. "You won't need it any longer."

To my relief, she began unwrapping Verdy. Agnes came to help, taking the cloak as Edith held Verdy to her chest.

"Have you done what you came to do?" Edith asked, stroking Verdy's back. "Have you saved Tom? Will he come back, so she can meet him?"

I didn't know what to say. I couldn't tell her everything would be all right. In war, nothing is ever all right.

"I don't know about Tom," I said, "We came to save you and your baby. Tom will take care of himself. You need to start living. For Verdy. But continue to hope."

I turned away, and was glad when Agnes held the cloak out because my eyes were filling up and it drew attention away from me while I wiped at them with the back of my hand. Both Frank and Major Billings's mouths dropped open, but they said nothing.

After that, there were hugs, handshakes, and a few salutes. Maggie handed Annie something wrapped in a cloth and me, Mitch and Annie picked our way through the tangle of burned beams and rubble. When we got to the fireplace, Annie and Mitch said a sappy goodbye, so I turned to give them some privacy. Maggie, Agnes, Frank, Major Billings, and Edith and Verdy, were in a line, standing by the side of the lane, with a clear view. We had never before had witnesses to our departure, and I wasn't sure how that would go. Were they going to stand there until we fell asleep? That could take a long time. And what if other people came by? Would we draw a huge crowd? That was not our intention.

The intent was to allow those who believed—that we were criminals, angels, or foreign spies—to see the truth. Once they knew, once they could not deny what they saw, our secret would be safe. Leaving them with their suspicions meant that rumours about us would grow and take root. Once they knew, once their suspicions were satisfied, they could make peace with the truth, and let any stories about us fade.

That was the idea, anyway.

Behind me, Annie was begging Mitch not to go, or to take her with him, and he was explaining that he couldn't do either.

"It doesn't work like that," he said. "We both need to go, and nothing from here can travel back with us."

I turned to face them. They were still in a loose embrace, but at least they weren't sucking on each other's faces.

"Look," Mitch said, reaching into his pocket. "I've kept your feather." He held it up for her to see. "It brought me luck, and I will hold it in my hand as we go, but it won't come back with me. It can't. And neither can you."

"Then I'll wait for you" she said. "I'll stay alive, no matter what, just like you did for me."

Then they started kissing again.

"We need to go," I said. "The sooner we start, the sooner it will be over. I don't know how long it's going to take to fall asleep. I don't exactly feel tired."

Annie took the cloth Maggie had given her out of her dress pocket and unwrapped a small, brown bottle.

"Ether," she said.

I shook my head. "That's illegal."

She held the cloth in one hand and poured a few drops from the bottle onto it.

"No, it's not," she said. "And I know what I'm doing. Now lay down."

We did. She covered us with the cloak up to our necks and kissed Mitch again while I looked away. We squeezed close, with our heads together, and she laid the cloth over both our faces.

"Until we meet again," she said, her voice thick.

Then she pulled the cloak over us, and everything went dark. It was time. I breathed in the sweet, chemical smell and relaxed. As I began to drift away, I thought about the box, Mom's cedar box that the bullet had been in. It was gone now, destroyed in the fire, no doubt, and we'd be in big trouble when we got back. Mom would accuse us of stealing it, which I suppose we had. It made staying in 1916 seem like a good idea, but as Mitch had explained, that couldn't be.

Then I felt myself slipping, spinning, falling into a huge, black hole.

Chapter 41
Thursday, 28 June 2018

Mitch

I opened my eyes. They felt as if someone had poured sand in them. My ears buzzed, and it took a few moments for the room to stop spinning. I didn't know if that was from the ether or the sleeping pill we had taken before we left. I knew we were back home because I was lying on a soft mattress and couldn't smell charred wood. I looked at Charlie, who was just waking up. On his chest was Mom's box, looking good as new. I flexed my hand. Annie's feather was gone.

I pulled the cloak off and Charlie groaned. Then he saw the box.

"We're in luck," he said. "If we can get this back in Mom's room before she wakes up." Then he shook it. Nothing rattled. His face went white. "There's no bullet. She's going to go mental."

"She can't accuse us of stealing it," I said. "There's no way we could have gotten into it. She has the only key."

Charlie sat up. "Well, what is she going to think?"

We decided there was nothing we could do about that, so we sneaked into Mom's room and, finding her still asleep, put the box on the bed next to her and the cloak back in the closet where she had hidden it.

It was a long day of waiting. When Mom got up, she breezed around the house, looking smug and satisfied. We tried to stay out of her way, but she kept finding things for us to do. I think she wanted to keep an eye on us, just because.

When Dad got home, she practically pounced on him. She made us all sit at the dining table and, holding the box in front of her, told Dad how his father had sent us a bullet.

"A bullet," she said again, but louder and with more emphasis.

Dad bobbed his head. "Yeah, I agree. Sending a bullet is out of line. I'll contact him and tell him not to send anything like that again."

"He'll send nothing," Mom said, practically shouting. "He will stop sending all these ... these gifts. Nothing more. Nothing at all."

Dad bobbed his head again and seemed to shrink. "Look, if my father really sent a bullet, I'll—"

"If," Mom shouted. "If? I have it right here. I'll show you what your father sent, and you can tell him he's not allowed to send anything else."

With that, she held up the key, unlocked the box and flipped if open. Then her face went white, and her jaw dropped.

Charlie and I sat still, trying not to give anything away. Then Dad asked her what was wrong. Mom didn't say anything, she just made a sound like "Ahhhh," and shook her head slowly.

Dad gently slid the box away from her. I couldn't understand why, having seen the box was empty, she didn't accuse us of stealing the bullet. Then Dad, who was staring into the box with a puzzled expression, reached inside and pulled out a white feather.

269

"It was a bullet," Mom said. "A bullet. A bullet. A bullet."

It became a chant, repeated over and over, as she rocked in her chair, not looking at anyone.

Dad looked at the feather, then at Mom, his eyes wide, his face etched with confusion.

I got off my chair and went to Dad, who was now staring at the feather. It was getting uncomfortable, and a little spooky, listening to Mom repeating "It was a bullet," over and over, and my stomach was in knots because I felt so bad for her.

I plucked the feather from Dad's fingers and held it up, turning it, inspecting it. It was the feather Annie had given me in the Carfax, in Horsham, three thousand miles away and over a hundred years ago. I put it in my pocket, went to Mom and gave her a hug, holding her to make her stop rocking.

Then I turned to Dad and said, as much to Mom as to him. "It really was a bullet."

Epilogue
August 2018

Charlie

"You need to see this," I said to Mitch.

I was in the dining room, looking at my laptop, having brought up an archive of the West Sussex County Times.

Mitch came in from the living room.

"What?"

"I've been trying to see if I could find evidence of a Zeppelin attack on Horsham, so we could know if we were really there or not."

"But I do know," Mitch said. "I have Annie's feather."

It was true, he did; he kept if on his dresser and fondled it every morning. I was surprised it hadn't been worn down by now.

"That's fine for you, but I want something more concrete. And I think I found it."

I turned the screen so he could see the article I'd just read:

The Miracle of the Angels

When Edith Pike's husband, Sergeant Thomas Pike, was listed as missing and presumed dead, she never gave up hope. Her daughter, born after her father returned to France, was named Verdun, after the battle where he was thought to have died. Mrs. Pike was understandably distraught. But then she was visited by two angels.

"They came the night of the Zeppelin attack," she told this reporter. "My cottage was bombed and burning. They appeared out of the smoke and led me to safety, then rescued my daughter. No human could have survived that inferno, or appeared like that just when I needed them."

Mrs. Pike claims that, when the angels left, they told her Tom was alive, and promised he would return home one day.

Mitch looked up from the screen. "We did no such thing."

"Just read."

This inspired Mrs. Pike to join the Woman's Army Auxiliary Corps when it was established in February 1917. She furthermore joined the Suffragist movement and involved herself in raising money to buy clothing for solders on the front lines. But all the while, she continued to believe the angels.

Two and one half long years later, in March 1919, and against all odds, her husband returned.

He had been wounded, taken prisoner, hospitalized with the Spanish Flu, shuffled between Germany and France, and eventually ended up back in Britain.

"It was a miracle," Mrs. Pike said. "The angels watched over him and delivered him back to his family, just as they promised."

All this happened ten years ago. Thomas is fully recovered and working on the Shaw farm, Edith remains involved in local charities, and Verdun is a bright girl following in her mother's footsteps.

And they all, to this day, continue to believe in the angels.

"That's good her husband came back," Mitch said, but it's just a lucky coincidence.

I nodded. "Yeah, but check out the picture."

Beneath the article was an old sepia-coloured photo with a caption reading, "Could they be the angels?"

The photo was of Edith's house on the morning after the raid, with a crowd of people staring at the smoking rubble.

"Look there" I said, pointing to two figures in the background.

It was unquestionably Mitch and me, staring straight into the camera. Even though we were dressed in Agnes Shaw's son's clothes, we still looked out of place. And out of time.

"Those reporters," Mitch said. "They did take our picture."

"This article proves we really, truly were there," I said, only now fully understanding the difference between believing and knowing. It wasn't pleasant.

"What are you going to do?" Mitch asked.

I closed the browser tab, clicked on settings, and deleted the browsing history.

"Make sure Mom never sees it," I said.

Historical Note

Zeppelins really did cause havoc with the British morale in the early days of World War One.

For the first time in history, the British were not safe in their island fortress, and the supposed invincibility of the Zeppelins gave a large part of the population many sleepless nights. The Germans hoped the Zeppelins would cause such panic that the British government would pull out of the fighting and leave the French on their own on the Western Front.

However, Lieutenant Leefe-Robinson, using a combination of Brock, Pomeroy and Buckingham ammunition, brought down Zeppelin Schütte-Lanz SL 11 in the early hours of 3 September 1916.

This is a truncated version of his official Account:

September 1916
From: Lieutenant Leefe Robinson, Sutton's Farm.
To: Commanding Officer No. 39 H. D. Squadron.
Sir:

I have the honour to make the following report. On the night of 2-3 instant. I went up with instructions to patrol between Sutton's Farm and Joyce Green.

On the whole it was a beautifully clear night. I saw nothing until 1.10 a.m., when I picked up a Zeppelin S.E. of Woolwich. I made for the Zeppelin, hoping to cut it off on its way eastward, slowly gaining on it for ten minutes.

I flew about 800 feet below it from bow to stem and distributed one drum among it (alternate New Brock and Pomeroy). It seemed to have no effect.

I therefore moved to one side and gave them another drum along the side, also without effect. I then got behind it and by this time I was very close—500 feet or less below—and concentrated one drum on one part (underneath rear).

I had hardly finished the drum before I saw the part fired at glow. In a few seconds the whole rear part was blazing. When the third drum was fired, there were no searchlights on the Zeppelin, and no anti-aircraft was firing.

I quickly got out of the way of the falling, blazing Zeppelin and, being very excited, fired off a few red Very lights and dropped a parachute flare.

Having little oil or petrol left, I returned to Sutton's Farm, landing at 2.45 a.m. On landing, I found the Zeppelin gunners had shot away the machine-gun wire guard, the rear part of my centre section, and had pierced the main spar several times.

I have the honour to be, sir,

Your obedient servant,

(Signed)

W. Leefe Robinson, Lieutenant

No. 39 Squadron, R.F.C.

Robinson was awarded the Victoria Cross for his heroics and became an overnight celebrity. He saw further action in France in 1917, where he was shot down and taken prisoner.

He returned to England in December 1918 and died of the Spanish Flu on the 31st of December.

About the Author

Michael Harling is originally from upstate New York. He moved to Britain in 2002 and currently lives in Sussex.

Lindenwald Press
Sussex, United Kingdom

Printed in Great Britain
by Amazon

60513547R00163